CAPTURED ON CAMERA
A PARKER PHOTOGRAPHY COZY MYSTERY

SUZANNE BOLDEN

Published by Laughing Deer Press

Cover design Molly Burton www.cozycoverdesigns.com

❧ Created with Vellum

CONTENTS

CHAPTER ONE

*C*hicago in my rear-view mirror was just what I needed today. My breathing eased as her skyscrapers faded from view and sprawling suburbs filled with office complexes, giant warehouses, and subdivisions appeared. I took the Kennedy Expressway out of the city. By the time the farm fields west of Chicago were in view, I was totally relaxed.

When I'm in town, my home is a loft in River North. I rarely drive in the city, because one thing Chicago gets right is public transportation. My SUV is primarily used for these road trips to southwestern Wisconsin. Getting behind the wheel and heading to my hometown of Harmony is my favorite road trip. I skirted around the south side of Rockford before heading north to the peace, quiet, and calm of the small town life I grew up with.

I'd flown into Chicago's O'Hare airport ten days ago from a photo shoot for a luxury resort on the coast of Croatia. Since then, I'd done two charity events, back to back. I donate my services to causes I support and the organizers of these events love that. They get excellent event photographs free, and they publicize the fact that world famous photographer Jacqueline Parker will be in attendance to capture the event's festivities as only she can do...or some such hyperbole. In certain circles I have gained a degree of fame, and if that helps bring in more cash donations, I'm glad. But chasing around to capture the who's who in Chicago society trying to make sure they were photographed with the right people, isn't my favorite thing.

I'm grateful to have this getaway to look forward to. A little grounding in the reality of day-to-day life for most people always centered me. I could count on my Aunt Ruth to bring me back to earth if I ever started exhibiting of what she termed highfalutin mannerisms.

This was going to be a special trip back to the village of Harmony, because I'd be working with my aunt again. She and Dad took over the family business, Parker Photography, from their father. At one time people who could afford the cost of posing for formal portraits at important touchstone moments in their lives like confirmations, graduations, and weddings flocked to Parker Photography. It was the only game in town and we were good at what we did. Like so many businesses, time brought change. Our family photography studio saw fewer and fewer bookings. Dad and Ruth tried to adapt and did okay with the outdoor casual photographs that families favored. High school graduation was a big deal, and most students booked sessions with Ruth. But the advent of digital and social media meant an easier entry point for new photographers and thus more and more competition for Parker Photography.

A month ago, Aunt Ruth had asked me to help her with photographing the Sunday afternoon wedding of one of Harmony's own social elite, Eleanor Harmony. The oft married widow was vowing to love and honor yet another husband. When Aunt Ruth reached out to me for an assist, I was happy to help. Ruth and my father were the ones who inspired me to become a photographer. They guided me through learning processes, encouraged my eye for capturing an image at many levels, and instilled in me a sense of independence. I built on what they taught me and now enjoyed a financially comfortable and interesting life because of it.

I rarely photograph weddings unless it's for a close friend or an outrageous fee these days. I smiled at the memory of shooting the wedding of a country music star and her manager popped into my head. Such a fun weekend. Ah yes, there was that handsome cowboy who wore his hat with just the right tilt. What a night of stomping my lizard skin cowboy boots in rhythm with hundreds of others, line dancing on that Nashville dance floor...

Oops, almost missed the turnoff! Pay attention, Jackie, I scolded myself. I stopped at this spot every time I came home. Sunshine or rain. Night or day. This point was where I caught my first glimpse of the Village of Harmony nestling against the Wisconsin River's edge and extending up into the forested area called Harmony Hills that rose around it. Home...this would always be my home, though Chicago was now my base. When someone from another state or even another country asked me where I'm from, I'd most often say Chicago. The mention of it was always good for a conversation starter. People recognized the name. Odds were that they themselves had been there, or they knew some who had. They'd nod and mention a restaurant they've been to, or how they loved the view from Sears Tower. I never corrected them to call it Willis Tower, because I've been calling it Sears Tower myself ever since Aunt Ruth took me to see it as a child.

But Harmony was home, my true north.

The river shimmered in the spring sunshine as it bent and twisted, running past Harmony Hills on its way to the Mississippi, just as it had for thousands of years. This area of Wisconsin was named the Driftless Area. Glaciers from the last ice age stopped short of scouring and flattening the landscape here, leaving rolling hills and forested ridges, deep river valleys and spring-fed streams.

I have countless shots taken from here over the years. In all seasons and all times of day. Hmm, maybe a coffee-table book one day? I'd have to consider that. I love introducing people to the geographical beauty of our earth. I've also taken hundreds of photographs of goodbyes when I leave Harmony. Waves from Mom and Dad now both gone, and goodbye waves from Aunt Ruth...the constant in my life.

I jumped back into my car. Time to get going, Ruth would be waiting on the curb outside the studio on Main Street. We were scheduled to meet with the bride-to-be today.

Little did I know how the next three days would change things for Eleanor Harmony.

And for me.

*S*ure enough, there was Ruth with her big smile. "Hello Jackie!" Ruth said as she opened the car door. Settling herself in, she gave me an air kiss before snapping on her seatbelt. "Isn't it a glorious day though?"

"The best." I checked over my shoulder and pulled out. So little traffic here compared to Chicago's streets. "We haven't worked together since I was a kid. This should be fun. Where does our lovely bride-to-be live?"

"She's up in the old Harmony mansion. Do you remember it? Her parents used to throw elementary school picnics there when you were in grade school."

"I do remember that. Cool place. All us kids were so impressed. The stables with those beautiful Arabian horses! And if I remember right, there was something like a petting zoo? I had nightmares of being nibbled on by baby goats afterward, though. Oh yeah, and the squealing pigs, I can't forget that sound."

"You were not a farm child, that's for sure," Ruth quipped. "Don't forget the bunnies. Everyone loved the bunnies! Okay, take a right on to Harmony Hill Road. The house is at the top, you'll see the big stone piers at the entrance. I'm glad you came a day early to get the lay of the land. The ceremony is scheduled for early afternoon tomorrow on the north lawn. Eleanor wants us to shoot some interior shots beforehand, too. I've got a feeling it's because she'll be moving out soon."

"Staying in the area though?"

"Yep. I heard the newlyweds are moving to the Mill House. The original home place for the first Harmony family to settle here. Right near the site of the original lumber mill."

"So who is she marrying this time? And remind me what happened to the ones who came before."

Ruth chuckled. "Well, now. First one was someone she met in college. She went out East for college, which was rare in those times for the local families. But they got married here in Harmony. It was customary to hold the wedding in the bride's hometown, you see. Guess Eleanor and her father both had visions of hubby taking over the lumber business, but that didn't work out. Eleanor tried living on the east coast for a while, but she was quite the Daddy's girl and returned home without husband number one in tow."

"Divorced? That would have been unusual then too?"

"I suppose so. But Eleanor weathered all the gossip. She really loves this village, and gets her hair done with all of us at the Cut-n-Curl," Ruth said.

"Does Val still run that? Gosh, I'd love to catch up with her while I'm in town."

"She sure does. And she's as fun as ever." Ruth paused, and I caught her quirky little grin out of the corner of my eye. "Though I retain a few memories from your high school years involving you, Val, and Wanda making questionable choices. Nonetheless, you all survived and thrived."

I had to laugh. "Questionable by your era, but not for kids growing up in the 60s and 70s! Okay, back to husband number two."

"He was a local doctor. Eleanor's parents were still alive, and the doctor didn't want to move into the mansion with them. The newlyweds moved into that original, smaller home down the hill, the Mill House. He passed away after about three years. Strange case. He contracted a horrible infection in a wound. Guess he thought doctor, heal yourself. By the time he agreed to take it more seriously and went to Northwestern in Chicago, it was too late. But I remember the funeral. Big event. After that, Eleanor again moved back into the mansion with her parents. Turn here, Jackie."

I remembered this entrance. Gigantic oaks edged the sides of the paved driveway. "So, this one is her third marriage?"

"Nope, it's number four. I'll tell you about number three later. After we do our location shots. I see Eleanor up ahead," Ruth said, pointing me toward the mansion. "And it looks like her fiancé is here too. Come on Jackie. Game on!"

CHAPTER TWO

"*P*aul Griffin? Is that you? What a small world!" I exclaimed.

The man's eyes narrowed as he tried to place me. Figured I'd get him out of the awkward moment by extending my hand. "Jacqueline Parker. I believe the last time we ran into each other was at a charity event at McCormick Place a couple of years ago."

He extended his hand to me. "Of course, now I remember! I'm so sorry, Jacqueline. Was it for the Northwestern Hospital Charity event?"

"You know I don't remember myself, so don't feel bad. Plus, you're quite a well know figure in the social life of Chicago and meet so many people. You might not remember me as I was probably there in a professional capacity."

Eleanor Harmony patted his arm. "Now isn't it a small world, dear? Jacqueline here is a famous photographer. Her aunt has asked for her help in capturing our nuptials on camera. Now why don't you run along, Paul? I have thousands of things to take care of."

"Of course. Tomorrow's our big day." Paul turned to me and smiled warmly. "I may have been what you say I was at one time, but right now my future is with this lovely lady here in Harmony. Nice to meet you, Jacqueline, and you as well, Ruth."

Paul gave Eleanor a hug and a quick goodbye kiss. It was nice to see them finding each other late in life. I found myself curious how Paul and Eleanor met. I must ask Ruth after she fills me in on husband number three.

Eleanor shouted to a group of young guys rolling racks of white folding chairs. "Not there!" She turned to us, shaking her head. "Excuse me a moment. These youngsters apparently don't know that the flowered arch is where I will walk through. Not the altar where we take our vows." She grinned and gave us a thumbs up. "I'll meet you in the front by the main staircase in a minute." Then she scurried off to handle chair arrangements.

"So welcome to bedlam," Aunt Ruth said. "I advise you to take a deep breath and wait for her to show us what she wants."

"But I thought you wanted me to come and help? To offer my input on the places to take photos."

Ruth put her elbow through mine as we strolled toward the house. "I do. But I'm giving you a heads-up about Eleanor. She likes to micromanage. Prepare to gently offer your suggestions. And Jackie, part of why I wanted you here, besides enjoying my favorite niece and her expertise, is that I didn't know if I was up to handling this big of an event by myself anymore. Did you know your father and I photographed all her weddings?"

"I didn't know that. But don't be silly! You've done countless weddings. It must be engrained in your brain by now."

With a pensive nod she said, "I suppose it is. But my brain is old. Nice as Eleanor is, I don't know that I can deal with her like I did before."

Her tone of resignation struck me. "Where's Mandy? Your new assistant you were so encouraged about?"

"She's been a godsend. So bright and energetic. Smart as a whip, too. Creative. Inspiring."

"Ruth, that's great. Why isn't she helping you with this event? I mean, I'm glad to come and it'll be fun to work together with you, but why not Mandy?"

"She's on her honeymoon."

I gently stroked Ruth's hand resting on my arm. Her

skin was dry and thin. I felt the delicate bones in her hand. Funny how people you see often rarely seem to change. Then there comes the time it catches you by surprise. Maybe it was what she just confided in me, that she was feeling less secure about her abilities, that made me recognize the signs of her aging that I hadn't noticed before. Heck, I thought, I do it to myself too. Turn my eyes away from my signs of aging, like how I try to avoid a mirror after a shower. I let out a soft, self-deprecating chuckle.

"What's so funny?" Ruth asked.

"I was just thinking how great you look at your age. You have such beautiful, delicate hands. Remember Val used to tease me about my farmer hands?"

"Pshh…powerful hands are a sign of…or was that big hands? Hmm? I can't remember what the saying is."

I burst out laughing. "It might not be a saying about powerful hands that you're trying to recall." I couldn't be sure Ruth heard the joke about the size of a man's hands relating to another part of his body, so I ended it there.

"Darn, it's the one about a man's hand size and his…" Ruth smacked her hand over her mouth.

"Ruth Parker!" I acted all aghast at what she had just said. "I never…"

Her eyes were twinkling above the hand covering

her mouth. A few smothered snorts leaked out before she burst into full out laughing.

I jabbed Ruth with my elbow and tilted my head as Eleanor approached us. Ruth took a deep calming breath and straightened her shoulders, giving me a wink.

"Welcome to the day before the wedding madness!" Eleanor said.

"Looks like you are in control of things. Now where is that staircase you wanted family photos on tomorrow?" Ruth said.

Eleanor led us inside the mansion and stopped at the base of an elegant curved staircase. "Isn't she a beauty? I wanted to use this for some shots in case the weather doesn't cooperate."

"It's gorgeous," I said. "I'd love to set up some photos here, even if the weather is fine. Do you have some other favorite places in the house? A wedding is the perfect time to record those memories too."

Eleanor thought a moment. "That's not a bad idea, Jacqueline. Especially since we'll be moving to the Mill House. Yes, let's do that. I'd like a photograph in here," she said as she pushed open a heavy door with ornate dimensional carving in its panels. "This room empowers me. It was my father's office and I still find a quiet strength when I'm in here."

"What a wonderful testament to him," Ruth said.

I pulled out my Nikon. "The light coming through those tall windows might be perfect. May I open the drapes to take a couple of photos?"

"Any other rooms you'd like us to photograph?" Ruth asked. "I remember a stunning solarium at the back of the house where you used to hold garden club meetings. The wicker pieces and all the greenery would be a terrific backdrop."

It was nice to see Ruth's creative juices flowing. After consulting with Eleanor about her vision for our work tomorrow, we stepped back out on to the wide expanse of the mansion's front porch.

"I would like some shots that include the river if that's possible," I said to Eleanor. "This is such a beautiful view."

Eleanor seemed to hesitate before saying, "Jacqueline, I'd like you to be very conscious of the landscaping when you frame the shot. I'm afraid the crew I frequently use, had a hard time completing their work on the grounds in time for the wedding. Things seemed to have been overlooked."

I agreed with her. I'd noticed the ragged appearance in the landscaping. Overgrown shrubs looked to be a year or more behind in trimming. Flower beds contained questionable greens that pushed the limits of what I might consider a modern trend called wild grasses. Looked more like good old weeds or lawn grass gone wild. "Of course, Eleanor. We'll keep that in mind."

Ruth asked, "Does old Tom still work for you?"

"He does. But I'm afraid his days of maintaining the grounds for this entire sprawling estate are past."

"I remember seeing him at the nursery picking out some flowers a few weeks ago. He remarked about brightening things up for the nuptials."

"Paul and I have been looking forward to this day. It crossed my mind that for my fourth marriage perhaps I should have just gone to a Justice of the Peace," Eleanor said as a small chuckle escaped her lips. She wrapped her arm around Ruth's elbow. "I wanted you to be the photographer on my last and final wedding day. The fact I'll be moving out of the mansion and settling with my honey in the cozy little Mill House, made the decision to throw a party here easy."

"Once things get going, you'll relax and have a wonderful day. You always do," Ruth said.

"What time do you want us here?" I asked.

"I'm going to be at the Cut-n-Curl in the morning for a 10:30 appointment, Jacqueline. Can you be up here at let's say noon? We can take some interior shots then and family photos after the wedding. There shouldn't be too many of those. I only have Chelsea and several cousins."

"Please Eleanor, call me Jackie. See you tomorrow at noon."

The arrival of a florist van with *The Flower Girl* written proudly on the side quickly distracted Eleanor. "Katie does the best flower work. Just look at those Irish Belles and how she pulls in the white Lisianthus. Gorgeous."

"You haven't lost your eye!"

"Just my stamina!" Ruth said.

I took a few more photos around the grounds. It always helped me to see places through my lens. To see how they appeared in a photograph, the angles, light, and shadows.

On our drive back to the village, Ruth shared the story of Eleanor's third husband, George Grimshaw. "He was a local man who worked for Eleanor's father for a good many years. I think old man Harmony thought the gods had been kind to him. He'd get the son, albeit through his daughter's marriage, that he never had. Someone to give the family business to."

"But why didn't he have Eleanor take over? I mean, she's smart, went to college, and seems like a take charge kind of person."

Ruth shrugged. "I don't know. Even though Eleanor

was always her daddy's princess, I doubt he ever seriously considered her running the business. That's the way it was for many women of our generation. And to be honest, I too have a hard time picturing her running a lumber company. George, the new husband, was put in a tough spot. Working at a company starting to go downhill, like other lumber businesses in Wisconsin. George Grimshaw convinced Frederick Harmony to shift to making pallets because the type of wood required was still abundant around here. But it turned out to be a big gamble that failed. You should see the piles of old wood pallets stacked up on the grounds of the lumber yard up the hill where George set up operations."

"What happened to him?"

"He ended up hanging out at Shorty's tavern most every night. After Eleanor's parents, kind and decent folk, died in a car crash on their way back from spending the winter in Arizona, things continued downward. George died in the mansion. Rumor going around was that it was by his own hand. I've always thought he fell down that enormous staircase and broke his neck. Whichever, he was gone and Eleanor was all alone. She took back her maiden name, and that was that."

"Who is Chelsea? Eleanor mentioned her as part of the family."

"Eleanor and her second husband had a son. Sadly, he died young in a car crash on one of our many winding roads. Chelsea is his daughter. Pretty girl. You'll meet her tomorrow. Now, let's get you settled and head out for supper."

CHAPTER THREE

*E*arlier today I'd been excited about seeing Ruth and didn't take in the fresh coat of paint the studio received. I looked at the facade with fresh eyes. It needed more than paint. It needed a complete overhaul.

Growing up and spending time in this studio, my attention had been on other things. Like, would Dad let me arrange the setting for the baby photo session today? Could I make goofy faces to get her to smile? How about if we changed up the light angle? What the building itself looked like hadn't been my focus then.

Ruth was excited to get the place painted. She told me it brightened up the shop, which I suppose it did. Other storefronts along Main Street ranged from those with *For Lease* signs in the window, to used but half functioning ones like the station down on the corner with its gas pumps gone, to fully restored beauties like an antique shop across Main Street from us. So yes, it was better than nothing, but…

"I love the paint colors you chose for the facade of the studio. Looks like other businesses are stepping it up a notch, too."

In traveling for my work, I get to see many parts of the world. From ghost towns and abandoned mining sites in the Rocky Mountains to a recent business trip to Ireland's west coast to photograph ruins of castles and old forts there. At least Harmony wasn't going down that path to abandonment. To becoming a ghost town. People loved it here on the river. They were going to do what it took to keep their village in good shape.

"Thanks, Jackie. It did need a bit of sprucing up, I will admit. Didn't Hannah do a top-notch job with your mom's old dress shop?" Ruth pointed across the street.

"Wow! That's so cute! When did that happen?" My mother, who always dressed impeccably, owned the local dress shop when there were such things. Before the big department stores, and catalogues, and eventually online shopping changed how small-town retail looked. She loved to go on buying trips to Chicago when the new season's fashions came out. Mom had such great taste in clothing. She brought in merchandise that the ladies of Harmony and the surrounding area would flock in to see. I remember her fussing over each customer, bringing out garments that she thought were perfect for them. They often walked out with her yellow and white, eye-catching shopping bags in hand.

Devotion to fashion wasn't my thing. I was always hanging around the photography studio. And my choice in clothes ran to whatever Mom put in my closet. But now I realize I still like those simple, classic styles she picked out for me. Of course, Mom kept updating my wardrobe. From plaid jumpers over blouses with Peter Pan collars in grade school, to A-line dresses and pleated skirts with slim turtleneck sweaters in high school.

"Hello Jackie! Earth to Jacqueline!"

"Oh sorry, I was lost in the 60s and 70s, remembering how Mom dressed me back then."

"You were her little mannequin. With your slim frame and height, I know she often thought you might go into modeling."

"Seriously?"

"Yep, but not you. You weren't a tom boy, but you just never had her same passion for fashion!" Ruth said. "But back to Sutton Antiques. I love the job their contractor, Scott Drake, a Sam Elliott lookalike if I may say so, did with the restoration of it. We all got grants from village funds to spruce up our storefronts. Hannah went above and beyond with her antique shop. She's been in there a few years now, but this update really catches the eye. Great addition to Main Street."

"So, did you get a grant too?"

"Sure, but I didn't want to sink a lot of effort, time, and money into this old beauty. They'd have to approve this and that. Like the balcony up there. It's probably not up to code."

"I love that balcony! They could grandfather it in. I mean it's so, oh I don't know…necessary!"

Ruth stepped back to the edge of the sidewalk and looked up at the small balcony. "You're right. It is. If the powers that be are aiming for an artsy and cutesy vibe, that little Juliet balcony definitely fits the bill."

"Who is this *they* you're talking about?"

"The current board members. All this fixing up on Main Street would be a good draw for tourists, they say. Only way we'll survive as a village, they say. I say…I need an Old-Fashioned! Let me take you out to Wildwood Supper Club."

"Sounds good to me. Can I leave my photography gear in my car?"

"I'd bring it inside." Ruth turned the key to the front door of Parker Photography. "I think my only hope of keeping this place much longer is turning it into one of those dress up in antique time clothes and take a photo kind of joint," Ruth said as she turned on the interior lights. "Or I might try to sell it. Getting too old for this. And for the climb up the stairs to the apartment."

Her words surprised me. Just as the fragility of her hands had earlier. Was she really getting too old to keep doing this? I loved the creaks of the old wooden floor, so familiar and welcoming. I breathed in the smells of the oil soap Ruth used to clean the floor and the lemon polish on the counters.

She couldn't sell. This was her home. And mine, too.

Setting my camera gear case down behind the front counter, I watched Ruth climb the stairs up to her apartment. I'd have to talk to her more about her future plans. But right now, a cocktail at the best supper club in southern Wisconsin sounded perfect. I hurried up after her with my luggage.

From the top floor there was a view out to the marina, the river, and the hills that rose beyond on the other side. From here I could see the wide part of the river, also known as Lake Harmony. Looking left I saw the local tavern, Shorty's, neon sign flicker on. I remember trying to sneak in with my friends. Big bellied grouchy old guy owned it then. I wasn't very good at doing sneaky stuff, so my acting all grown up didn't impress him in the least. I can still remember the snorts and shakes of heads as I slid off my barstool and slouched out the door after they called my fake ID. My friend Wanda, however, took her time leaving. Checking her lipstick in the mirrored back bar. Patting her bouffant hairdo, before blowing a kiss to the bartender and joining me on the sidewalk. I can still remember the bartender's belly laugh at her audacious behavior. God, I had some fun with that girl!

"Ruth, the Wildwood is west of town, right? I'd like to stop in at the Riverview Motel. Wanda should be done with her remodeling of it."

"Sure, Jackie. She did a terrific job getting that old place ready for those tourists the wise people of this town claim are coming." Ruth's tone of cynicism couldn't be missed. I'll get a drink in her and things will smooth out.

The motel and small cottages were stunning. Their simple white paint on the batten board exteriors was perfect, and the rich blue trim and shutters cozied up the exterior. White shaded lamps hung above each motel room door, pushing a soft glow down to the walkway. Small porches with white wicker furniture and window boxes filled with spring blooms decorated the cottage units. A white picket fence had been installed at the edge of a small lawn with a flagstone path to the motel office. This had been an old decrepit SRO for years. The cabins occupied by long term renters. The place was rightly considered an eyesore for anyone entering town from that direction. Now it was gorgeous!

I noticed that several of the cars in the parking lot had Illinois plates. Maybe some of these people were in town for tomorrow's wedding. The woman at the front desk, wearing a tag letting us know she was the Night Manager Nadine, said Wanda wasn't in. "Can I help you with something?" she asked in a pleasant tone.

"I'm just an old friend and wanted to see her new place here. But my aunt and I are headed out to supper, so I'll try to catch her another time."

"Should I let her know you stopped by?"

"Sure, thanks." I pulled out a business card and handed it to her. "I'm in town for a few days so I'll leave a message on Wanda's phone."

"Enjoy your evening," Nadine said, waving as we left.

I quickly sent off a text to Wanda letting her know that I was in town and would love to get a tour of her new establishment.

The Wildwood Supper Club had a lively Saturday night crowd. We put our names in with the hostess and found a seat at the bar.

"Hey Ruth. Long time no see. Whiskey Old-fashioned sweet?" A middle-aged woman with vivid blue eyeliner and an easy going manner asked as she wiped the area of the bar in front of us.

"You bet. And see what my niece here wants, too. You remember Jackie? Joanna and Bob's daughter?"

"Ruth, you know that was before my time! But nice to meet you, Jackie. What can I get you?"

"I'll make it easy on you and have what my aunt is having. Excuse me." I reached into my purse to pull out my cell phone. A text from Wanda!

Hey girlfriend! Sorry I missed you.

I responded. *In town to shoot a wedding. Can we get together?*

Go for a hike in the morning?

Sounds great. Where at?

Path leading out from behind the motel is great. See you at 8?

See you then.

"Sorry for the texting, but that was Wanda. We're going for a hike tomorrow morning. I'll be back in plenty of time to get us up to the wedding."

Ruth was just shaking her head. "I'm so behind on using cell phones. Texting, messaging, face watching or whatever they call all that."

The bartender put our drinks down in front of us and said, "These are on Wanda."

The puzzled expression I felt squishing up my face was wiped away by someone reaching around and covering my eyes. "Guess who?"

"My knight in shining armor?"

"No. Guess again."

"The horse he rode in on?"

"Hey! Do these manicured beauties feel like hooves?"

As soon as I said, "Wacky Wanda!" I found myself engulfed in a great big hug from my high school locker buddy and lifelong friend.

"You sure had me going with those text messages!" I said.

Wanda looked the same as always. I swear she just didn't age. A big smile, a twinkle in her eye, and that wonderful casual no fuss look about her. How did she still have that kind of mojo going?

Wanda agreed to join us for dinner. We sat at a table with a view of Lake Harmony. We all ordered the prime rib special and as typical in a supper club, nibbled on the items in our relish tray while we waited for our meal.

The evening flew by with conversation and laughter. Ours was one of those friendships that transcends time spent apart.

However, our laughter and chatter meant Ruth drank one too many Old Fashioneds, and I had to help her up the stairs to the apartment. She was softly snoring by the time I sank into my nest on the sofa. The windows were open to the night breezes. Good to be home I thought as I dozed off.

CHAPTER FOUR

anda and I had been hiking on the path that wound its way up the wooded hill for just a few minutes. The Sunday morning light filtering through the young spring leaves was magical, and the air held a cool bite. I was the first one of us to notice a glare, a sharp bright reflection of the sunlight bouncing off something in the hill above us.

But it was Wanda who pushed through the underbrush to find out what it was, saying, "For heaven's sake, can't people pick up their trash. So help me if I find out who dumped something up there I'll have their hide."

I watched her weave through the trees and low brush as she climbed the steep angle. Ever since I battled a severe case of poison ivy from a teenage adventure that ended up off the beaten path, I tended to stay on trails.

The young me lacked will power because the admonitions of don't scratch it went unheeded. I itched and scratched to my heart's content. It was awful! My mother had to practically tape my hands to together to make me stop. Eventually, after four miserable days, I ended up getting medication. Not something I wanted to experience again, so I waited for her on the hiking path.

That is until Wanda unleashed a piercing scream.

I charged up the hill to find her.

The car she stood by was leaning at an odd angle against the trunk of a young sturdy maple tree. Apparently, the tree had stopped the car's descent down the embankment from the road up above. Damaged saplings and bent shrubs marked the vehicle's path to where ended up, resting on its side.

But it wasn't the damaged car that brought on Wanda's screams and her shouts of, "Oh my god. Oh my god. Oh my god." It was the sight of a man's body in the driver's seat.

One of us would have to check on his condition and the way Wanda was going on I figured it would be me. After all being part of a crew in a war zone or at a refugee camp gave you a chance to steel yourself, prepare yourself, knowing there would be awful scenes you had to shoot. Walking up a hiking trail on a bright spring day in Wisconsin was not where I expected to encounter a death. At least one of a human. Maybe some roadkill, a dead squirrel or a...Okay Jackie stop thinking and get on with it.

I peered in through the glass of the windshield, but the deflated airbag blocked my view. "I can't tell. He might be just knocked out. There's some blood. Can't tell if he's breathing."

I knew the only way to get to the driver out would be through the passenger door. The vehicle's passenger side was slightly off the ground. It must have started to roll over, but the tree stopped it. The door was ajar. Maybe it sprung open when the car hit the tree. I hoisted myself up using the exposed undercarriage to get a foot hold. At that angle it was easy to see him.

He was dead.

His right eye stared up at me.

It was Paul Griffin.

I took a few seconds to capture my thoughts of Eleanor...wedding...tragedy...

Wanda knocked on the car hood. "Hey, mister. Wake up." Bang. Bang. Bang.

"Forget it. He's gone," I announced, before pushing myself back off from the car and landing on my butt in the tall grasses.

Wanda came running around. She offered me a hand

up. "He must have rolled down from the road. It can't be far above us," Wanda said.

"Can you walk up there and get a cell signal? Tell the police where we are? I don't know this area like you do."

Wanda's eyes darted back to the car, like a modernist sculpture installed here in the forest. Something an artist places in an unusual position...or in an unexpected place. This car sculpture fit both...unusual and unexpected.

"Hurry Wanda. Tell them we need an ambulance but request no lights."

"Right. No need to draw attention to this. I'll let the department know we'll need a tow truck too," she said.

I stood and pulled my cell phone out of the small leather pouch strapped across my chest. Besides the passenger door being open, there was something else that puzzled me about this scene. Just a strange feeling.

My early days as a crime scene photographer, taken to support myself in the big city, came back to me as I took several carefully chosen photographs of the scene. There was enough curiosity on my part to want to document this before the tow truck hooked on and pulled it out. Local police might not think to do that. Just figure the guy was drunk and ran off the edge of the road, flipping on his side and sliding to a stop. I try not to judge choices made, but quick decisions, like those often made by less experienced law enforcement, could lead to the destruction of critical evidence.

I hoisted myself up to look in the open car door again to take photos of the interior, including the position of the body. I photographed long scratches running on the side of the car. It looked like someone had sideswiped the car. Might that have caused the accident? Was there a guard rail on the road above?

Wanda yelled down to me. I could make her out between the trees and mangled scrub brush where the car had pushed its way down. She waved with big sweeping movements above her head. "They're on the way!"

I gave her a thumbs up and went back to photographing the undercarriage. I heard sirens. Oh well, I suppose that was protocol. Rooftops of an ambulance, a fire truck, a police car, and the triangular apparatus of a tow truck soon lined the roadway above. It must have been a gravel road because clouds of dust drifted up behind the stopped vehicles.

If this wasn't such a serious occasion, I would have laughed at the various styles of descent. A fireman chose a backward approach down one side where slender trees grew. He leaned in, grabbing the tree trunks as he descended. A tall gangly police officer did the sideways step, together, step, together method. Another officer stayed up at the top talking to Wanda. The tow truck driver had backed his truck into position to hook on and pull the wreck up so he actually did a repelling descent. Clever. Very good. Two EMT's, carrying a collapsed stretcher between them, managed a coordinated zig zag style descent.

The first officer pulled out his note pad. "I'm officer Patrick Murphy. And you are?" He stood poised pen in hand.

"Jacqueline Parker."

"I understand that you and your friend where hiking on the trail just below this point and noticed the vehicle? Is that correct?"

"Yes. We must have seen the sun reflecting off the windshield glass," I answered.

"It appeared the driver was dead when you arrived?"

"Yes officer."

Wanda and the other policeman had made their way down the embankment and were talking with a paramedic perched on top the wreck. He confirmed the driver's death just like me, by peering down into the car's interior via the open passenger door, because no one seemed to be in a hurry.

The tow truck driver arranged a harness that straddled the wreck. Apparently, he was going to get it upright that way. Would he get the car back on its tires to remove the body?

Wanda joined me and Officer Murphy as she asked, "Hey Murph. Did you run the plates yet? I don't recognize this car."

"I know him," I said.

"Hey Jeff, come over here. Jackie knows this guy!" Wanda yelled to the other officer.

"Hang on Wanda. I'm working here," he called back. "Tell Murph to call the medical examiner."

Wanda dismissively waved her arm toward Jeff, before turning back to me. "Who is it?"

"I just saw him yesterday. I believe the deceased is Paul Griffin. And it's his wedding day. I should say, was his wedding day. I can't be sure. I mean he's in a very awkward position."

Officer Murph seemed uncertain what to do.

"Let's wait to confirm until I can see his face," I said.

I watched the tow truck guy climb over the car, doing a last check before he started walking back up the hill. "Just give me a thumbs up when you're ready to have me turn it Chief," he called out.

"Ah, officer, don't you think you should get some photos first?" I asked Murph.

He turned and called over to his commanding officer. "Chief, lady here asked if we should take some photos."

"Hang on Murph." Jeff talked to the paramedics a moment longer as they set up the stretcher, getting ready to take the body out once they had access. The tow driver was back up top waiting on instructions. Jeff held up one finger to the tow guy showing he should hold on a moment.

He walked over to where Wanda, Murph and I stood. Now I saw he was a double for the actor Jeff Bridges. The lanky frame, graying goatee, and provocatively piercing eyes.

"Jackie, this guy is my cousin, Chief of Police, Jeffery Mathis. Jeff, meet my friend Jackie."

Okay then, nice coincidence. It'll be easy enough to remember his name!

"Nice to meet you, Chief."

He had that same cute grin as Bridges too. "Nice to meet you Jackie. Why are you thinking about photographs?"

"Just seemed like it might be good to do."

"Jackie is a photographer by profession," Wanda said.

Jeff nodded thoughtfully. "You're thinking like crime scene photos?"

"Well, sort of I guess."

"Not a bad idea." Jeff directed Murph to take photos

with his cell phone. "It seems clear what happened. The guy was run off the road or took a turn too fast. The car's body might provide evidence. We checked for any skid or slide marks, but that rain last night muddied up the road. The medical examiner will be here shortly to take a blood sample to check if drugs or alcohol were involved. Wanda tells me you two found the man and that he was deceased when you arrived on scene."

The tow truck driver shouted out again. "Hey you guys ready or what?"

"Relax Billy! Kids, always in a hurry." He turned back to me. "Now, I was asking…"

"Yes, I climbed up and looked in the passenger door. It was clear he had died."

"You opened the door? That must have been hard at such an odd angle," Jeff said.

"The door was open when we arrived."

What I'd just told Jeff piqued his interest. I figured it would. With a mumbled thanks and a tip of his police cap he strolled over to Murph.

Things had just changed.

CHAPTER FIVE

I picked Aunt Ruth up at the apartment. Since I'd met the deceased and had recent contact with Eleanor, Jeff asked me if I would break the news to her. It was an easy decision to take Ruth with me. This wouldn't be easy, and I was glad she agreed to go with me to share the sad news about Paul.

"On her wedding day no less." Ruth rocked her head slowly side to side. "I just can't believe it. This is going to be such a hit for Eleanor. The two of them were so cute together. Eleanor told me about their downsizing plans. In fact, I think Paul's been living at the Mill House when he's in town. Sense of propriety in her generation. Tell me again how you got caught up in this tragedy."

"By taking a walk with Wanda. We picked up a trail from behind the motel and up the back side of the hill.

Can you believe it? Good thing we saw it because it would have been hard to see from the road above. Where does that road go?"

"I think you were on the back road that leads past the old Harmony lumber mill. The old place she and Paul have been fixing up is off that road too. Here we are. I hope Eleanor hasn't left for her hair appointment yet."

"What's the old place?"

"Local name for the Mill House. The one I just mentioned Paul has been staying at. It was the original homestead of the Harmony family when they settled here. As their lumber business prospered, they built the mansion high atop Harmony Hill."

A caterer's truck stood near the back door of the mansion. A large white tent empty except for rolling racks of tables and chairs waiting to be set up. We pulled in toward the front where Tom was sweeping the front entry steps. He leaned on his broom handle and watched as Ruth and I got out of the car.

"Morning ladies. Lovely day for a wedding isn't it? Can I help you with something Ruth?"

"Morning Tom. Is Eleanor here?"

"No, she left early for her hair appointment. Chelsea took her in. She even got Eleanor to agree to have her makeup done today too. They left earlier than expected."

"Tom, excuse me, but did Paul return here last night?

We saw him leave when we were here in the afternoon. But might he have spent some evening time here with Eleanor?" Ruth asked.

"What are you suggesting by such a question? Eleanor never let Paul stay overnight. Young people might be into all those goings on, but no..."

"Oh my gosh no Tom, don't get your knickers in a knot. I meant nothing like that." I saw Ruth rolling her eyes and shaking her head. "I was just wondering if they might have enjoyed an evening nightcap or something."

"When he left in the afternoon was the last time I saw him." Tom gave a final quick whisk of the porch steps. "Need to do some work out back." He hurried off.

"Well I put my foot in that didn't I?" Ruth said. "I was going to give him a heads up about Paul's death, but he got his dander up. He's been a protective constant in Eleanor's life."

"Then we should let him know."

"No, we should get to the Cut-n-Curl and tell Eleanor the bad news before word spreads."

"You're right. I forgot how fast news travels here. Let's go."

The downtown area was Sunday morning quiet. But through the window of the Cut-n-

Curl I saw Val working on Eleanor's hair. A young woman, sitting in a chair near the door, had her nose buried in her cell phone. She jumped when the bell above the door jingled as we walked in. Must be Eleanor's granddaughter Chelsea.

"Why look who the cat dragged in!" Val held her comb up in the air as if saluting our entry. "Jacqueline Parker if you aren't a sight for sore eyes." She scurried over and gave me a big bear hug.

"Good to see you old friend," I said.

"Old? Keeping my roots a stunning auburn color is supposed to make me look young. Now if I could go gray like you gorgeous lady, I would. I can tell you get your hair done in one of those big city salons. No way that a dark brunette would gray without it looking obvious. And your hair looks stunning."

I was feeling uncomfortable with Val rambling on about my hair when I knew what we were about to tell Eleanor who waited patiently in the salon chair.

"Val, we have something to talk to Eleanor about. Some sad news," Aunt Ruth said in a soft somber voice.

That caught Chelsea's attention. Her finger rested on her phone screen, but her eyes were on us.

Eleanor raised her gaze to the mirror in front of her and Ruth made eye contact. With a small downturn of Ruth's lips and a tiny shake of her head, Eleanor's expression changed. I watched a cloud cross over her face. This woman had heard a great deal of sad news in her life. And today, on her wedding day, we were bringing her more.

Val walked over and took the pink plastic cape off Eleanor's shoulders, freeing her to stand.

"It's Paul isn't it? He's not been well. His color has been so pale. He told me he was seeing a doctor in Chicago. That I shouldn't worry. Is he at the hospital in Greensville?" Eleanor's voice pitch rose with each word.

I stepped forward and encouraged Eleanor to sit back down in the stylist's chair. It swiveled slightly before I reached to steady it.

Chelsea and Val stood nearby, expectant.

Watching things unfold.

I knelt and spoke in a low voice, my hands resting on Eleanor's clasped hands. "I'm sorry. The last time I saw Paul he was so very happy. I could tell how much he loved you."

Eleanor's hands trembled. "Is he...?"

"He was in a car accident. He didn't survive."

"Oh god," Eleanor gasped.

Chelsea came and wrapped her arms around her grandmother.

"We met last night for drinks and to watch the moon

rise. Who would have imagined it would be our last night together?" And the first sob broke from her.

My ears perked up. Tom had told us that Paul didn't return to the mansion last night. Had Tom lied? Or was he just mistaken?

"Come on Grandma. Let me take you home now."

"Chief Mathis asked Jackie to let you know what happened partially because she discovered the accident."

"You did?" Eleanor said.

"Chief Mathis sends his condolences. He would like to talk to you later today if that's okay," I said.

"Of course, Jackie. Please have him call me."

Val stepped to the chair and put her hands on Eleanor's shoulders. "Let me take down your grand-mother's updo."

Eleanor shook her head. "No Val. I want to keep it up. You did a beautiful job."

Out of the corner of my eye I noticed the tow truck pulling Paul's wrecked car was driving past. Chelsea saw it too. She followed the awful sight with her whole body, shuffling slightly in an apparent attempt to block the view from her grandmother until it had passed even as she said, "I'm glad you're keeping your hair up Grandma, but we should get you home now. Maybe you want to lie down?"

Eleanor stood. "Jackie dear, I know this might be a

great deal to ask, but could you please check with the police and see what happens next? I know Paul has some relatives in Illinois. I must let them know. Oh and his business associate Alan Morris. He's in town for the wedding." She let out a sigh, then straightened her shoulders.

"Certainly Eleanor. I'm so sorry for your loss."

"Thank you." She hugged Ruth and Val before turning toward Chelsea. "I'm ready to leave now."

Val said, "Please let me know if there's anything I can do to help."

Eleanor said, "Thank you Val. I'll bring your payment in later."

"For goodness sake, Eleanor, you don't owe me a thing," Val said.

I saw Wanda approach as Chelsea and Eleanor stepped out to the sidewalk. She took a moment to take Eleanor's hands and speak a few words before heading in to the shop.

"Eleanor is handling this well. I'd be a basket case," Wanda said as she plopped down in one of the swivel chairs and began slowly spinning herself around. "The car's been taken to the garage. Billy said he'd tow it to the junk yard later."

Val said, "Now tell me everything! How did you two

find the wreck? What do you think happened that made Paul drive off a cliff on the old mill road?"

"Well it wasn't a cliff, more of a steep incline," Wanda said.

"I hope the police don't just think it was a run-of-the-mill accident though, no pun intended," I said.

"I'm sure they'll question the cause," Val said.

"I gave Jeff some of my questions. Was he side-swiped? Or did a deer run out? That can scare the bejesus out of a person. I had one jump out one time, my hood caught him at the bottom of his leap and that critter just boinked right back up off the car and landed pretty as you please on the shoulder of the road," Wanda said.

"Think I'll head back home. Maybe put my feet up for a bit," Ruth said. "It's been a long morning already. Jackie. Thank you for offering to help Eleanor deal with the police. That was nice of you."

"She asked you to help her? You two just met!" Wanda said.

Ruth laughed. "I think Jackie's the perfect choice. I'll bet she sensed how trustworthy and competent you are."

"Brilliant the way you slid that in Aunt Ruth. Make me feel needed. And I didn't offer, she asked."

"Does this mean you'll stay a little longer? Eleanor

will need help with arrangements and stuff. I'd help but I'm tied up here at the salon a lot," Val added.

Wanda threw her two cents worth in. "And I'd be happy to help, but the motel keeps me busy. Lots of stuff to get ready with tourist season right around the corner."

"And I was hoping you'd give me some ideas about marketing the sale of my photography business," Ruth added with a wink.

I threw up my hands. "Okay. Okay. I get the idea." I smiled at the group, eager expectant looks on their faces. "I'll stay a day longer."

CHAPTER SIX

The police station was empty when I got there.

"Hello!" I called. "Anyone here?"

I heard a flush, followed by the sound of running water. At least he washed his hands. Officer Murphy walked out tucking his shirt in his pants.

Awkward.

He hadn't heard my knock. "Sorry, I didn't mean to startle you. I called out but guess you didn't hear me," I said, averting my eyes.

"No problem ma'am. What can I do for you?" An embarrassed flush flared up his face.

"Eleanor Harmony, the fiancé of the car accident victim, asked me to talk with you. Find out what needs to be done. Things like that."

"Well now, not much right at the moment, I guess. The car's going to Cutter's Auto Salvage tomorrow. Old man wouldn't come down to open the gate for Billy. The body is...hmm I'm not sure where it was taken. Let me check with the ambulance company and find out." Murph picked up the handset and started dialing, then placed it back in the cradle. "Tell you what. The Chief just went for coffee and donuts for us. He'll be back in a minute. Why don't you have a seat and wait? I know he talked to the EMT's before they left."

"Did you pinpoint the cause of the accident yet?"

"Nope, but we saw some things on the vehicle that showed he might have been sideswiped. Or there's always the classic deer running out in front of the car. Or he could have just gotten caught in those soft shoulders this time of year. They'll suck you right in and send you rolling down quick as a hot knife through butter. Lots of reasons that cause the accidents. We might never know."

I had to push more. Was he showing signs of resigning himself to not finding out the cause? "True, things aren't always obvious. Do you have an idea what time it happened?"

Officer Murphy looked relieved as Jeff pushed the door open with his back and said, "Grace and Dermot make the best donuts this side of the Mississippi. They were out of the maple frosted though. Why look who's here! Good to see you again Jackie. How'd things go with Eleanor?" Jeff used the edge of the donut box to push aside papers on his desk. "Sorry I didn't know you were coming, or I'd have brought you a donut."

"She's doing as good as can be expected. My Aunt Ruth and I caught up with her at the beauty salon."

"Val was getting her prettied up for the wedding? Feel so bad for her. She's a strong woman, but this had to be a hard hit. Thank you so much for doing that. Much gentler than if I'd done it I bet. So, you're Ruth Parker's niece? She's such a sweetheart. Will you be heading back to Chicago now that the wedding photography isn't needed?"

"How did you know I live in Chicago?"

"Small town folks know lots of stuff," Jeff said with a grin.

"I might stay a day longer. For some reason, Eleanor asked me to help her, and I agreed. Doesn't she have family here? She must have a lawyer to handle things."

"Only family I know of is the granddaughter. She had one son, and he was killed in a car crash. You know if I remember right, it was on that same back road. And in the same stretch that takes that tight bend around the yellow stone outcropping. Poor kid, the mother abandoned her to Eleanor right after she found out her husband died."

That caught me up short. Not a nice small world moment. Two deaths there.

"Gosh why would she do that? That's awful."

Jeff took a bite of his donut, but leaned back and said, "Between you and me and the gossips in town, the woman was looking at being stuck with a young kid in a small town. Most people figured her hopes of inheriting the Harmony money went up in smoke the night Evan died. So she booked."

"Eleanor raised Chelsea?"

"Chelsea took it all unbelievably hard. Can you imagine knowing your own mother left you? Eleanor might have spoiled Chelsea. I mean she's the only grandchild Eleanor will ever have. Can't blame her. Now as to a lawyer, I'm not sure. There's a couple who still hang their shingles in town here." He shrugged. "Guess you'll have to ask Eleanor who handles her legal matters. How's she doing?"

"She's a bit shell shocked. Officer Murphy wasn't sure where they took Paul's body. Do you know? I'm sure that's a question Eleanor will have for me."

"They are holding the body at the hospital morgue in Greensville right now. Waiting on a call from Eleanor or his next of kin as to further arrangements." Jeff got up, brushing the crumbs off his uniform trousers. "Murph, I'm heading up to see Ms. Harmony and ask her a few questions."

"Sounds good Chief."

"Would you mind going with me up to the house," Jeff asked with a wink. "Seeing as she's kind of appointed you to manage things."

I gasped. "Manage things? Who said that? I just agreed to help a grieving widow. Well not a widow, I guess, but a grieving fiancé."

Jeff started laughing. "Just teasing you Jackie. Come on, I'll get you a coffee and donut and we'll drive up to see this grieving fiancé together."

I settled in the police cruiser with my coffee and a yummy Boston Cream donut for the drive up to the Harmony mansion. I'd met Grace and Dermot, proprietors of Murphy's Coffee Shop, and to my pleasant surprise, Officer Murphy's parents.

As we drove, Jeff and I went over a few things regarding the accident. "As to time of the mishap and death, the digital dash clock kept on ticking and the deceased had a very expensive watch that didn't stop during the accident either. I know that's always a good clue in murder mysteries, but no help here," he said.

"No time of death yet. I have conflicting information on when he left Harmony House. The gardener said it was in the afternoon, right after I met him. He was leaving to meet up with a friend who was in town for the wedding. But Ruth just said that he returned later on Saturday and that they had drinks together."

"We'll verify that time with her. And get contact information on the friend," Jeff said.

"Officer Murphy mentioned the car might having been side-swiped. Could that have caused the accident? My aunt thought Paul had been staying at what she called the old place. Is that located on the same road he'd been on?"

"Whoa there, sounds like I should be writing some of your questions down. Yes, to the damage on the vehicle looking like he'd been side-swiped. Could have happened recently. But hard to say it's what drove his car over the edge. And yes, the old place is on that road, sort of back way to the original lumber mill. Thanks for that information about him staying at the Mill House. I seem to recall seeing Scott Drake doing some remodeling work there."

"Eleanor and Paul were planning to move into the house. They wanted to downsize."

Jeff nodded. "Makes sense. And I've been hearing rumblings for months now that a resort group has been sniffing around Harmony. Maybe part of that moving story is that Eleanor is selling the mansion and the grounds to them. Sure is a beautiful, desirable spot up there."

"That would bring in more tourists," I responded.

"Has its good and bad points. Some in town are for it and some against it. Might have just been rumors, anyway. Giving hope to the council that the money they've been pouring into improvements will have been worth it."

CHAPTER SEVEN

The arrival of the Chief of Police's car at the Harmony mansion caused a few heads to turn.

"Looks like word hasn't gotten out to the guests yet," Jeff said. He put his police cap on and climbed out of the cruiser.

I pointed at the big tent where the setup crew was milling about. "Everyone's not sure what to do."

Cars that had followed us up the road to the house were being parked in an area designated by orange cones. Early arrival guests I assumed. What a sad day it will be when they're told the wedding will not happen and they turn around and go home.

I watched as Tom approached our car. He looked so confused. Ruth was right, we should have let him know about Paul's death earlier. He could have roped off the drive or something. Now it seemed things were spinning out of control. The stoic guests sitting in the fake wedding chapel's chairs made it look more like a wake than a wedding celebration, which in essence it was becoming unbeknownst to those still arriving.

"I'm so glad you're here, Jackie," Tom said. "Eleanor wanted me to keep an eye out for you. Afternoon Chief."

"Want some help to move the guests out of here?" I asked.

"Oh no. She wants them to stay. Said it'll help her get through the day. She wants to talk to people. Even plans on letting them have dinner or take the food home if they want. But she did ask me to bring you to her as soon as you arrived." Tom pointed across the lawn where Eleanor was speaking to a couple. "Doesn't she look beautiful? Even on such a tragic day."

Jeff and I approached Eleanor and waited respectfully to one side while she wrapped up explaining Paul's demise to a plump man and his equally round wife. They offered kind words of comfort. I've learned that many Wisconsinites are not into weeping and gnashing of teeth seen in some parts of the world and could be almost coldly stoic. Everyone knew someone who had been in an accident with alcohol involved. Though drunk driving had been cut back with the use of designated drivers, it was still a sad reality and might have caused Paul's accident.

Eleanor noticed us and excused herself from the two guests. She quickly explained her decision. "There was no way I could reach everyone on such short notice, so I decided to let them come. It's a beautiful afternoon and I have tonight to cry. But I'm at a loss as to how to manage this entire thing. I'm so glad you're here Jackie. You seem to have a good way of taking care of things. Maybe you can help me?"

Jeff choked back a laugh, but quickly disguised it as a cough. Not funny I thought. He knew what I'd been asked to do already. Including him asking me to notify Eleanor. I refrained from punching him in the arm. I came to town yesterday, met this woman, and now am being asked to change a wedding celebration into some sort of memorial?

"Did you find out where they've taken the body?" Eleanor asked.

"Yes. He's in Greensville right now," I answered.

Eleanor nodded as her eyes shifted to a handsome older man who had just arrived.

"We have a couple of questions for you, but this might not be a good time," Jeff said.

"Thank you for being considerate. I will answer

anything I can, but please give me a few hours with my friends."

"And I can help you with arrangements tomorrow Eleanor. No need to worry about it now. I'll let Greensville know to expect to hear from us Monday."

As the man approached, he reached out to give Eleanor a hug. "What's going on here? Why the long faces? Did the groom get cold feet?"

A collective gasp came from the older couple Eleanor had been talking to as they shook their heads and backed away.

The man noticed. He let go of Eleanor and looked around. He'd stepped into something he didn't know about. "What?"

I spoke first. "There's been an auto accident. The wedding won't happen today."

"Alan, I'm so sorry to have to tell you this, but they found Paul on the side of Harmony Hill this morning. He must have lost control of his car and crashed down the hill," Eleanor said.

"Is it bad? Will he be alright?"

I caught the man's eye and shook my head.

"No! this can't be. He dropped me back at my motel last night. He was so excited about today. To marry you Eleanor…"

Eleanor touched the man's arm. "He's gone Alan. We

are all trying to absorb it. I've decided to let the guests arrive. Their presence is comforting me. Jackie, this is Alan Morris, he's Paul's business associate and friend. Alan, meet Jackie Parker, my wedding photographer. And Jeff Mathis our local Chief of Police. They've been helping me this morning. In fact, it was Jackie who discovered the accident."

"What time did he drop you at the motel?" Jeff asked.

"Let me think," Alan said. "We left here around 10:30 right Eleanor?"

Eleanor nodded.

"But Tom told us no one was here at the house late last night," I said. "Could you have been mistaken?"

"Who's Tom?" Alan asked.

"He's my gardener and lives in that small cottage out back," Eleanor said. "He must not have seen us. Remember Paul brought you up here to enjoy a nightcap."

With a sad smile, Alan added. "Paul had his usual Mojito."

"He would have dropped you off at the motel and taken the back road to his house."

"The old place?" I asked.

"Why yess. That's what everyone calls it." Eleanor turned to point at the mansion behind her. "As opposed to this new place. New over fifty years ago!"

We all smiled at her remark. I was so glad I wasn't dealing with a sobbing puddle of a woman. I admired her decision to let things roll out as they would today. Like she said, time for grief would come.

Eleanor continued. "Paul and I decided that we would rehabilitate the old place, or as my family called it, the Mill House, and move there together. Smaller, cozier."

A man in a white chef's coat approached. "Ma'am. Please accept my condolences. I understand there has been a tragedy."

"Thank you. I realize you're concerned about your bill. I'll pay you in full of course. Even though some afternoon's festivities are canceled, could you please make plans for the food you've prepared to be served to the guests who are arriving? If you'll excuse me Jackie. I have a few things to attend to."

Eleanor was back in charge.

Alan said, "I'm booked at the Riverview for the night and I'd like to stay and help anyway I can. I'll start letting people and associates in Chicago know today if that's alright. Paul's been stepping away from the business side of things, but there will still be some legal processes that will have to happen as soon as possible. I hope you understand Eleanor."

Eleanor's face crumbled and her eyes moistened, but

again, she straightened her shoulders. "I understand. Thank you, Alan. I'm glad I can lean on you to help with those things."

As Eleanor walked away and Alan started to leave, I stopped him. "You mentioned Paul and you had drinks up here. Did you two have more to back at the motel?"

"Are you asking if Paul might have been driving drunk? I suppose it doesn't matter now, but he seemed just a little tipsy. We didn't drink more at the motel. And didn't have much here truth be told. I attributed it to him being tired, stressed with the planning. And my god but things get dark around here once the sun goes down." Alan took a deep breath. "I don't want to say it was just the alcohol, but perhaps poor eyesight? I must admit, having just learned this, that I should have insisted Paul not drive back to his place so late, especially because he was going up the back road, not the lined and paved road we driven on."

"Thanks for your thoughts Alan. Do you know the time he left you at the motel? And is there anything else you can think to share about last night?" Jeff asked.

Alan's face took on a thoughtful look, but he shook his head. "I don't recall anything remarkable about last night. Nothing out of the normal. As to the time, I can't say I looked. It felt like maybe a ten or fifteen minute drive. So, like 10:45? Was the accident near the motel?"

"Yes, it was. Just up above the Riverview, on Harmony Hill," Jeff responded.

"Jeff, since Eleanor asked me to help here with these rearrangements, would you consider taking me back to the accident site later? I'd like to check out that back road. The one Paul took from the motel."

Jeff winked at me. "Now I haven't had that kind of invitation since high school!"

I slapped his arm. "Chief, seriously?"

"Yep, best road with pullouts to see the city lights of Harmony."

"And I bet you got lots of cute girls asking you to take them up the back road," I said as I watched Jeff's face redden. "But trust me, I have a different motive."

Alan let out a laugh at my remark before saying, "Struck you down quick officer. Now if you'd please excuse me, I'd like to make a few phone calls if the signal is good here." Alan reached in his suit coat pocket and pulled out his cell phone, slipping away with a slight nod as he began searching the screen.

Jeff agreed to pick me up later this afternoon. I raced to catch up with Eleanor to find out where I was needed. I saw her waving me over and I ended up helping the caterers figure out a quicker buffet format instead of the plated dinner planned. Someone ran back to town to get chafing dishes and to-go boxes. The buffet line was soon in place.

As the time passed, I noticed Chelsea joined Eleanor in talking with the guests. Funny how knowing a little more of someone's backstory changes your view. Now to know Eleanor had been there for the young Chelsea, I could see time was reversing the favor.

Tom paced at the edge of the tent. "Do you think Eleanor is overdoing it?" he asked me as I walked over with an iced tea for him. "Sometimes there's just no telling her anything. This is the darndest thing I've seen. One minute a wedding event and next minute a wake, or whatever you want to call this. I'll see to it she lets me do all the cleanup when this event is over."

"Chelsea might be able to help with that too," I said. My curiosity about Chelsea and Eleanor's relationship prodded me to ask more. "I understand she's the last of Eleanor's family. That Chelsea's father died in a car accident? Is her mother still around anywhere?"

"I don't believe so. She left Chelsea with Eleanor within days of Evan's death and I can't say I've seen her since. She was a bit of a gold digger in my opinion. Got herself pregnant with Chelsea and when it was clear she would not be taken care of in the style she expected after Evan left, poof…she's gone too."

"That must have been hard on Chelsea. She was a young child?"

Suddenly Tom shifted the conversation away from the past. "Yes, but she's grown up and their relationship is good again."

"Most kids have rebellious periods. I'm glad they are doing well now. Looks like Eleanor will count on Chelsea more than ever," I said.

When things began wrapping up, I said my goodbyes and called Jeff to let him know I was ready to check out that back road. I had to smile because now I think I remembered it. The place teens went to do a little courting, with the romantic scene of the moonlit river and the twinkling marina lights below. Whew that seemed a long time ago.

As I walked out toward the front fence to wait for Jeff, I noticed Chelsea talking with a beautifully dressed woman with chestnut hair done up in a stylish bun. They were standing at the further edge of the yard. I waved, but she didn't see me.

CHAPTER EIGHT

*T*he first thing I noticed was a metal rim at the edge of the gravel road. Had the person who side-swiped Paul lost a rim in the process?

Jeff said, "That old rusty rim could have been laying there for months. To me it looks like the car slid down the hill doing a flip on to its side at the end. Not a high impact thing. The deceased was strapped in and the airbags deployed. In my estimation I'm surprised it killed him."

"So maybe he had a heart attack or something?"

"Sure, that's a real possibility. Oh forgot to mention, and I hope you don't mind, but when I caught up with Alan earlier, as it appears he was the last one to see Paul alive and to get contact information. I gave him your phone number so you two could coordinate things with

Eleanor. He seemed to think he could help with finding relatives. He said he'd reach out to Paul's secretary today."

"Not at all. In fact I'm glad you did. The tasks Eleanor sort of assigned me will be finished sooner that way. Jeff, did you check out the car for any mechanical issues that might have caused the accident? Maybe a failure of something that made Paul lose control?"

"I gave a quick glance, but I doubt it was that. And even if it was, not much you can do about it. The deed is done."

"I know but they like those things reported to the manufacturer."

We'd walked down the embankment to where the car had ended up. Jeff looked back up toward the road saying, "If it was something mechanical that caused the accident, it sure happened in the worst possible spot."

"I took some photos this morning. I suppose we could have a mechanic look if there's anything obvious on them.

"Hang on to those photos. Murph took some too, but I might want to see yours later. In fact, maybe Stu at the paper would like to use one or two. The famous Harmony Hills Happening's next edition is coming out on Tuesday." Jeff was kicking at the brush in front of him. "Why is it you're so interested in this accident? I mean you didn't know the guy."

He bent to pick something up.

"My natural curiosity. I'd met him in Chicago before, too. My immediate goal is to give Eleanor the cause of the accident before I head back to Chicago."

"Look what I found. A key to the Riverview. Did Wanda drop it when you walked here yesterday?" Jeff asked.

"We met up in the motel office so Wanda might have been carrying one."

Jeff slipped the key into his pocket, just as my cell phone rang. Apparently, someone gave the morgue in Greensville my phone number as a contact. I explained I was locating next of kin and would get back to them.

I'd just hung up when I got a text message from Alan. *Hi Jackie. I wanted to let you know that I reached Paul's family in southern Illinois. They'll take over arrangements from here. The body is being picked up from Greensville ASAP.*

"Well that was quick," I said. "A text from Alan saying Paul's relatives are taking over from here. Oh darn, I didn't get contact information for the relatives."

Jeff said, "And I'm sure Eleanor will want to know who these people are and what their plans will be.

As I texted Alan back to get a name and phone

number to give Eleanor I asked, "Will the autopsy even be done by then?"

"I don't know if they planned on doing one," Jeff said with that shrug of his.

"No autopsy? Isn't that normal procedure? Like to rule out a heart attack?"

"Not always. Depends on the circumstances. The cause of death would seem to be the impact. They would have done blood work to see if alcohol was involved, but beyond that..." Jeff started his shrug again, then he paused. "You know what Jackie, the more I look at this..."

I watched as Jeff dialed his cell and snapped off directions to Murph to get hold of the Greenville coroner and make sure an autopsy was being done.

*A*fter Jeff dropped me back at Ruth's apartment, I was more than ready to chill for the rest of the evening. We walked to the park on the river with glasses of wine and watched the setting sun's reflection on the water. The marina lights were flickering on and wonderful smokey odors of grilling wafted across to us. Slow oldies floated out of someone's speakers.

"What a day," Ruth said. "Thank you so much for stepping up and helping. How is Eleanor doing?"

"She seemed to have a few difficulties but was handling things alright, I guess. Jeff drove me by the accident site. Such a sad thing to die like that. All alone on the eve of your wedding. I wonder if someone else was involved. Maybe sideswiped him and sent him over the edge?"

"Well if that happened the person surely would have stopped to help Paul," Ruth said. "I can't believe any of the good people in this town would have left him there alone like that. Nope, I don't buy it."

Part of me agreed with Ruth, but I said, "Even small towns have bad apples."

"Of course, they do. But Jackie, small town living has been good to me. I love it. I've traveled enough, nothing like you. Goodness, what country haven't you been in? But for me the familiarity is a great comfort at this point in my life. Sometimes there's a poignancy about all the change going on around here, but I try to be pragmatic. Change is constant."

There was a peace that washed over me here too. I'd traveled the world, and I wasn't ready to stop, but I could see it happening at some point in my life. Where would I end up?

"Well dear girl, time we went back," Ruth said. "I'm glad you're staying tomorrow. Wish you'd stay until Wednesday when Mandy returns from her honeymoon."

"I'll be back soon Ruth. You know I can't stay away from here long."

We strolled back up across the darkening park and on to Main Street, where lit lampposts created a charming small town street scene.

"Is the story about Parker Photography's original owner including that little balcony for his wife true?" I asked as we approached the studio.

"It's what I've always heard. They came from a German village where that was common. I have a photograph of the family standing on the balcony above their stationery and bookstore," Ruth replied. "And I have other photographs too. I wish we had a local historical museum to showcase Harmony's history or it will be lost."

Later, sitting in the evening's darkness on that second-floor balcony built by a German's love for his country and his wife, I watched the moon rise. From a walk with an old friend to discovering a fatal auto accident to managing a wedding reception turned on its head, it's been a busy day.

How long should I stay? I didn't pack much. I pulled out my phone to confirm that my calendar was free. Just a few unscheduled obligations, things that I could put off. I'd see how tomorrow went.

While in my phone, I tapped on my stored photos to

glance over the ones from the accident scene. What was I expecting to find? Don't go looking for trouble Ruth used to tell me.

I decided that on my way to Eleanor's tomorrow I'd stop and introduce myself to the editor of the Harmony Hills Happenings like Jeff suggested. Let him use one of these if he wanted. Oh, and maybe one of the staging photographs from yesterday? Those were such beautiful vistas from atop Harmony Hill.

Down the street the local bar was quiet. The red neon OPEN sign was still lit, along with Old Style and Pabst Blue Ribbon signs hung in the dark windows. Did they even still brew those beers?

Billy must still be working with someone at the old gas station on the corner. Inside lights burned while silhouettes moved about. The tow truck with Paul's car still attached was parked along the dark side of the building.

What would tomorrow bring?

CHAPTER NINE

When I was growing up in Harmony, the newspaper took over an entire building on Main Street. Now the Harmony Hills Happenings headquarters had been relegated to a small office next to Murphy's Coffee Shop.

A coffee and one of Dermot's donuts might be in order when I finished here. I tapped on the window and Grace gave me a wave from behind the baked goods glass display where she was helping a customer.

The sign in the window at the paper's office read, *We'll be back soon please step inside!* Stuart Walters, as his desk plaque announced, appeared to be the sole staff for the Happenings publication. It surprised me that the publication still existed. I checked out the photographs, diplomas, and awards framed and hanging on the surrounding walls. Photographs of not only events here in Harmony, but personal ones as well. Stuart was quite socially active!

I didn't recognize the people he was posing with, but each photo showed a beaming Stuart. In many of them the woman I saw talking with Chelsea yesterday appeared. She was just as striking and stylish in these photos as what had originally caught my eye. Must be his wife.

A jovial man hurrying through the front door startled me. "Why hello there! Hope I didn't keep you." He thrust his meaty hand toward me. "Stuart Walters at your service."

"Not at all." I pointed to the bakery box in his hands. "From Murphy's?"

He pulled a chair out for me and opened the box. Perfect! I reached for the maple frosted donut nestled in among several others. Stuart had already set a full coffee cup in front of me.

"Welcome to the headquarters of Harmony Hills Happenings, the reader's choice for information on all things happening in Harmony!" He set a bowl of creamers and sugar packets down and took a seat in a chair on the other side of a well-used desk, evidenced by the scarred surface and remnants rings of past coffee cups.

"Oh my. This is quite a welcome. Do you treat all walk-ins this way?"

With a hearty laugh he said, "Try to please the public and support local businesses." He clasped his hands across his notable belly. "And then there's me! I get the leftovers."

"Well this public person appreciates it very much. Thank you."

"You must be Jacqueline Parker. Jeff mentioned you might come by with photos of that sad and horrific accident yesterday. Poor Eleanor, after living with that awful clumsy last name of Grimshaw for years she was finally going to get a good solid sounding last name of Griffin. Don't you agree?"

I had to laugh. "Mr. Walters, I believe she goes by her maiden name of Harmony."

He held up his hand. "Now stop there. Call me Stu. Everyone from around here does. And I consider you a local gal, even if you only visit occasionally." He leaned across his desk. "I love your work. May I call you Jackie?"

"Certainly. But how do you know me and my work?"

"Harmony is a small town." Stuart said with a wink and a grin. "I know your Aunt Ruth very well. She's a good citizen. But getting up there in years. I'm surprised she's been able to keep up with the photography work.

She made a wise move hiring Mandy. Smart gal. Saved the day for her. All the new technology takes some learning, and it's not always easy. Take me here at the newspaper. You might wonder how I manage." He waved his hands across the room as though there was an entire press room of staff surrounding us. "But enough about that. Let's see those photographs. Imagine, a J.P. Parker image in our paper. Quite an honor for me Jackie."

Stu rattled off an email address to send the photos to and within seconds was peering at them on his computer screen. In this business he's forced to move forward into the digital age to survive. He was intent and focused, remarking on the things I'd chosen to photograph.

"This damage to the driver's side, was that caused when they righted the vehicle?"

"Caught my eye too. It looked to me that it happened before the accident."

"I agree." He zoomed in on the image. "Come around here and look at this. See that color there?"

I could see what he was talking about. There was a small amount of a vivid blue left in the scrape. Debris and dirt from the slide had partially hidden it.

"I'm glad you use high resolution to take photographs, even on your cell phone, or we might not have seen this." He aggressively tapped the screen with his finger. "I'll bet you ten to one that came from Edward Gray's pickup. Old beater of a beast. Can't believe he painted it this god awful color. Think he even did it with cans of spray paint. He went off the deep end when he lost his business a while back."

"Do you think they maybe met each other on that narrow road and Paul lost control of his car?"

"Possible, I guess. Ed probably had his usual buzz on and might have been driving drunk. But I can't imagine him being on that road. Most often he just leaves the bar and heads home to the trailer park outside of town. But not to say he didn't encounter Paul somewhere else. Ed is a bitter angry man. And one target of his anger is Paul Griffin." Stu leaned back in his chair.

My ears perked up at that. "Seriously? Why on earth would that be?"

"In his mind, Ed blamed Paul for his own failures. Paul and his partners invested in Ed's company and Ed took the money. When the company turnaround didn't come, he wasn't happy." Stu shook his head. "You know how those things go. But old Ed never accepted it was his own failings as a businessman that played the biggest part."

"That would explain him being angry with Paul," I said.

"Did you know it was during those times that Paul and Eleanor met?"

"I didn't! I can imagine that knowing Paul was going to be living around here would drive Ed especially crazy."

"I would suppose so. I guess the reporter in me, and I was a good one back in the day. Wasn't always a small-town paper publisher you know. Anyway, the reporter in me thinks this might be something worth considering. Ed could have seen Paul driving by in that fancy car. Could have been stalking him. Feel my blood pumping Jackie! Did I tell you I was an investigative reporter?"

"No, you didn't. That must have been so interesting." I felt I'd better slip away soon, or I'd never get to Eleanor's. "Please feel free to use any of the photographs you want. Just please, not any of the graphic ones out of respect for Eleanor. The last ones were more overview shots from when I was up on the road, those might be good ones."

"Why thank you. I'll assign attribution to Jacqueline Parker. I'd love to do an interview with you if you're in town for a while." He looked up and with a wave of his arms read the headline he was envisioning. "Local Girl Makes Good. We could write about you learning from your aunt in the family photography studio. In fact, we could do a live interview on the Happenings Facebook page. Or do a question-and-answer kind of thing."

"Whoa Stu. I may be in town for an extra day, but I don't think anyone cares all that much about me."

"Nonsense. Plus, it would be a good boost for Parker Photography! We could offer a coupon or something like that."

"I take it you're the marketing man for the paper too?"

Stu chuckled. "I wear many hats."

I stood and thanked him again for his hospitality.

"I'll be checking out Paul Griffin to get some extra facts to add to tomorrow's story," Stu said.

"That's the investigative reporter in you. I'm off to Eleanor's. She asked me to help with a few things."

"Can I ask you to get a brief statement from her? It would personalize the story. Hey, but how do you know her that well?"

"I don't know her well Stu. I've just happened to be in a position to help. I'll ask her if she wants to comment. Catch you later. Very nice to meet you!"

With that I made another commitment.

I have to learn to say NO.

CHAPTER TEN

The sky this morning was an indescribable blue. Try as hard as I could, I never seem to find the perfect word to describe things like the color of this sky. Instead, I take photographs to capture nature's beauty. I envy a friend who's a successful author. A wordsmith. A poet. He'd know the right words. He once told me that my photography gives viewers an experience, same as his poetry does. You just create that sensation in a different medium he explained.

Jeff told me that the road the accident happened on, wound its way past the old house and the entrance to vacated Harmony Lumber Mill property. Then continued on to a back entrance to the Harmony House and grounds. I decided I'd take that path to visit Eleanor instead of driving the paved county road.

The road left Main Street just past Wanda's motel so I pulled into her parking lot, intending to ask her about the motel key card Jeff found at the accident site.

"Morning girlfriend," Wanda said. She stood behind a white bead-board front desk checking out guests. "Grab a coffee and meet me out front."

Can't have too much coffee was my motto.

The motel grounds straddled Main Street with lodging on one side and river access on the other. At this point Main Street was turning into just another road out of town. I crossed the road and sat in an Adirondack chair. A row of the colorful chairs were artfully arranged to capture the best views of the river. Spring color from scattered daffodils and hyacinths brightened the scene. A few kayakers were out enjoying the calm waters. I could see why Aunt Ruth loved it here. So did I, but after a few days I knew I'd be itching to get back to work. I loved my work. It brought me satisfaction and joy. What I'd done to build my brand and my business left me financially comfortable. The slow quiet pace here in Harmony Hills felt wonderful. I was glad I always had it to come to.

"Can never get enough of glorious morning sunshine on the river." Wanda said as she joined me. "We'll be seeing the hummingbirds return here soon. I just put out their special feeders this morning. The guests just love them! And yes, you may set up your camera and capture the birds on film my hot shot photographer friend. I'll have them framed for my guest rooms."

"Hey, I don't remember asking you that!"

Wanda punched my shoulder. "You didn't. I was kidding. But I am planning on some new promotional materials and would love to hire you to do the photography. I've always dreamed of a seasonal calendar featuring this property. We could pull more tourists in for the fall colors with some luscious, tempting photos by J.P. Photography."

"Wanda, the hummingbirds maybe, but a seasonal calendar? That would require a great deal of travel and time on my part. To capture things at their peak."

"Exactly! You'd be here more often for us to see each other! You've not been coming around as much as I'd like."

"You can visit me in Chicago you know. The city is stunning. And I'd be your personal tour guide. Taking you around to museums, showing off our lake front, and of course, sharing the nightlife."

"You're right. I need to expand myself. Last time I was there it was with John. Gosh, I miss him! We started this motel rehab project together. It was going to be something to keep us busy in retirement. An investment for our old age."

"How long has it been since John's passing?"

"Almost four years." Wanda's eyes misted up as she let out a sigh. "But I think he'd be proud of what I made of the place."

"He would Wanda," I said. "I'm very impressed with what you've done. Now let the tourist traffic come!"

"How's your day going? I understand you and my cousin were wandering around on Deadman's Curve last night."

"Deadman's Curve? Where did that name come from?"

"It's what it'll be called now that a second fatal accident happened there. Did you know that Evan, Eleanor's son, died on that same spot? Someone will think they see a ghost trying to return to his love Eleanor waiting at the altar. Kids will drive slowly by, telling tales of death and spirits, trying to scare their friends."

"Don't be morbid Wanda."

"Jeff stopped in this morning." Wanda leaned closer toward me. "You two discovered something while you were investigating there, didn't you? Come on, share."

"Did Jeff show you the key card he found? Do you think you might have dropped it while we were there yesterday?"

"He brought that up. I use the programmable key cards but can't read the data once it's on the card. I did have two guests requesting new cards yesterday. Said they misplaced their cards. One was a family traveling to Michigan. They thought one of the kids had lost it. The other was a guy who'd been hiking. So I told Jeff that was probably what he'd found."

"And you would be the only one who knows about guests reporting lost keys?"

"Well, no. I do have someone available 24/7, my assistant manager Nadine. You met her Saturday night. I can ask her about it if you think it's important. What are you and my handsome cousin thinking might have happened to Paul? Come on spill the beans. I can keep a secret."

"We're not sure. Just a few odd things that make little sense. Jeff hasn't even questioned Eleanor yet. She was so worn out last night. I'm headed up there now and Jeff was planning to meet me there. So maybe he'll have something more to tell you later. And I need to let her know that Paul's family from southern Illinois is claiming the body at the morgue in Greensville."

"Really? Is the autopsy done already?" Wanda said. "That was fast."

"That's what I thought. But other than bloodwork to check for alcohol levels they might not have done an autopsy. But Jeff requested one so he should get the results tomorrow."

Wanda shook her head and pinched her lips. "Sometimes, I swear, people just figure things are what they appear. I love a good mystery story where things are never as they appear. And I know you're feeling it too Jackie, aren't you?"

I nodded in agreement. "Alan said Paul brought him back here to his room before heading home. Alan thought maybe Paul got confused on the dark road, or the alcohol got to him. Guess the blood work will shed some light on that."

"Who's Alan?"

"Paul's friend and sometime business partner from Chicago. He came in for the wedding and mentioned he was staying here at the Riverview. I think he was leaving today."

"Now I know who you mean. Handsome man, slight limp…caught my eye," Wanda said with an exaggerated wink. "He checked out late yesterday afternoon."

"Well, I'd better get going. I'll keep those ideas about promoting the motel in mind. I haven't seen the river with the fall colors reflected in it in a very long time."

I slowed as I approached the big rock outcropping. What Wanda now called Deadman's Curve. It wasn't far until I came to signs saying no trespassing. Jeff had warned me about these. They were posted to discourage hunting. Eleanor abhorred it, though her own father had gone on big game hunts around the world. Jeff told me to just keep pushing through along the gravel road and you'll come out at the back side of the mansion grounds.

Portions of the Harmony Lumber Mill were located on the river, but they had long ago been torn down and the land sold. Eleanor still held the land I was traveling on now. During Ruth's accounting of Eleanor's previous marriages, she'd explained that up here were remnants of husband number three's ill-fated endeavor of manufacturing pallets.

I was curious the Mill House, the home being remodeled for Eleanor and Paul to move into. It came into view at the end of a long drive. I saw why they wanted to live here. The setting was stunning. A grove of white birch trees and huge oaks threw dappled shadows on the wild grounds around the house. An old apple orchard nestled up against a simple wooden fence near the weather worn house. Even with the abandoned sense that hung over the house and grounds, I could see what she had been. The front porch steps sagged and the flagstone leading to them was almost buried under tall grasses. Simple, classic farmhouse style.

Scaffolding hugged a stone chimney where a workman was tuck pointing, repairing the mortar that held the stones together. Three pickups and a squad car were parked in the back. I could hear power saws and hammering coming from inside the house. The remodeling was still in full swing.

I saw Chief Jeff talking to a man with a logo on his blue denim shirt. He must be the contractor doing the work here. I didn't mind waiting for them to finish as these men were both easy on the eyes.

But Jeff noticed me pulling in. "Hi Jackie! What are you doing here?"

"Morning Jeff. I'm heading up to question Eleanor and thought I'd come this back way to check out the old place."

"You just missed Chelsea," Jeff said. "Eleanor sent her to gather up Paul's belongings."

Jeff introduced me to Scott Drake, the contractor. "Sorry to hear about Paul," Scott said to me. "He seemed like a nice man. Are you the go between with Mrs. Harmony about our work here?"

"Oh no. Eleanor just asked me to help her out with arrangements for Paul's funeral. I'm on my way up there now."

Scott reached into the back pocket of his jeans and

handed me two of his business cards. "Please give her my card and mention that I'll keep working unless I hear different. And if you'd please keep the extra one just in case you need to reach me."

I remembered Ruth saying he looked like Sam Elliott. I had to agree. Especially the low sultry tone of his speech. And then that gray mustache and the graying hair at his temples. I'll gladly keep your card I thought.

"Jeff, why are you here?" I asked as Scott walked back into the house.

"Just earning my salary," Jeff said with a grin. "I had a couple of questions for Scott. How long are you in town?"

"I'll probably leave…"

"Yoo-hoo!"

I nearly jumped out of my skin.

"Hello there! What a busy place!"

Jeff's eyes rolled back in his head as a woman stepped out of the new white luxury SUV and approached us. He leaned over to whisper, "Meet Kim Walters, biggest flirt in town and most aggressive realtor. I'm out of here." He turned to wave to Kim, calling out, "Hey Kim. Catch you later. I'm in a hurry."

Kim appeared much younger than her husband Stuart. The sunlight on that chestnut hair made it glitter with streaks of gold. Her figure-hugging peach colored sheath was a stark contrast to my denim jacket and white button-down shirt. But at least my leather flats handled this uneven gravel better than her four-inch heels.

CHAPTER ELEVEN

*H*armony House was quiet. In the distance I
saw Tom come out of a gardening shed
pushing a red wheelbarrow full of bags of fertilizer. The
world had tilted off its axis yesterday, but this must be
what a typical spring day at Harmony House looked like.
The big tents were gone, the flower draped canopy and
altar had been removed. It felt like a fold in time had
formed, covering the recent past.

Jeff pulled in ahead of me and was waiting on the
front walkway. "Are they expecting us?" he asked.

"I called Eleanor when I left Riverview. Wanda
mentioned you stopped in and asked her about the
motel key card you found at the accident site. You know
they've already started calling it Deadman's Curve?"

Jeff said, "No kidding? That sounds like my cousin. I learned you two were great buddies back in high school."

"We were and I still consider her my best friend. When we get together, it's like no time has passed."

"You're quite the world traveler. She rattled off a few places you've been. I'm impressed," he said.

"I am lucky to do what I love and see the world in the process. And I'm also lucky to have been raised here in Harmony. Hey, did you visit Harmony House with your grade school classes? I remember doing that. It impressed us kids."

"I still am impressed," Jeff said with his cute shrug. "I have a memory of Tom being here, maybe the wheelbarrow is new, but…"

Chelsea stood on the porch and waved us to come inside. Eleanor waited in a wood paneled study with a rich smell of old leather and new lemon polish. Lilac scents drifted in through the open windows behind her. She graciously offered us iced tea from a pitcher on the side table as we sat down on chairs arranged near an enormous wooden desk.

I told Eleanor about Paul's family taking over the funeral arrangements. "Plus, I have two things people have asked me to convey to you. Stuart Walters would like a statement from you to include in the Harmony Hills Happenings Tuesday addition. Scott Drake asked me to let you know he'll be continuing on the rehabbing of the Mill House unless you direct him otherwise." I slid Scott's card across the desk where Eleanor was seated. Chelsea remained standing with her back to us as she looked out across the lawns.

"I'll call Stuart and contact Scott. Thank you for being such a help to me. Have you discovered what caused Paul's accident?" Eleanor said.

"May I answer that?" Jeff looked at me before continuing. "I've ordered an autopsy, but until we learn more, it was probably a combination of tiredness, old eyes, and a dark night. But I need to ask, do you know of anyone who would want to harm Paul? We found an unusual scrape on the side of his vehicle."

"I'm glad Jackie's involved in your investigation Jeff. I felt that she was brought into my life for a reason. As to someone wanting to hurt Paul, the only person who comes to mind is Edward Gray. He used to have a business in town. Paul's firm thought the business warranted making an investment in. In fact, that's when Paul and I met. I remember him telling me later that he thought Mr. Gray understood the risk when he took the money, but he blamed Paul for his business failing. Mr.

Gray has been very vocal about it to other people in Harmony and word has gotten back to me. Are there any other questions?"

"When was the last time you saw your fiancé alive?"

"When Alan and Paul left at 10:30," Eleanor said. "He was going to drop Alan off at his motel. I'm not sure which road they took going into town, but he would have taken the back road home to Mill House. If that's all I'd like to share something that my dear grand-daughter Chelsea has brought to my attention."

Jeff nodded.

"As I mentioned to you earlier Jackie, this was my father's office and I find it gives me strength. He was the one constant man in my life. As you perhaps know Paul would have been my fourth husband. People may laugh to think of someone marrying this late in life, but I embraced the dreams Paul, and I had for spending the rest of our lives together. I asked my granddaughter to gather up his things from the old place and bring them here. In the items she removed from the house we discovered these."

I noticed Chelsea's down turned eyes as she stepped away from the window and put her hands on the back of her grandmother's desk chair.

Eleanor slid several sheets of paper toward Jeff and I.

"They are medical records from Paul's Chicago physician. He had begun transferring things to the doctor here in town as we planned on making this our home base. Paul did not share with me the concerns he'd expressed to his doctor about these recent bouts of diarrhea and nausea. Chelsea helped me research those symptoms along with another strange one. Both of us noted that Paul's breath often smelled like garlic."

Jeff asked, "What are your concerns about this? Do you think it has something to do with the accident?"

"It appears Paul was exhibiting signs of low-grade arsenic poisoning. And yes, he could have had an episode alone in that dark night that caused his car to leave the road," Eleanor said, with a catch in her voice. "Chelsea would you continue for me?"

What Eleanor told us shocked me. "Where on earth was he coming into contact with that?" I asked.

"That's what Grandma and I have been trying to figure out. According to the records, it's been going on for about three months, which coincides with him spending more time here," Chelsea said. "The only plausible way would be through something at Harmony House. My grandmother exhibits no symptoms and her and Paul have been enjoying meals together most every day."

Eleanor took a deep swallow and said, "My granddaughter has jumped to a conclusion which I find baffling. That someone has been poisoning Paul? In fact, she thinks she knows who it is. Let me say upfront I do not agree with her, but I must let her speak of her concerns."

Chelsea stepped from behind the desk chair and stood to one side. Releasing a deep sigh she looked Jeff and I directly in the eye and held our gaze.

Eleanor reached for Chelsea's arm. "Wait! Please let me say one more thing. I don't want to think that what my granddaughter is about to tell you could be true. But I'm not naïve and I think you two should look into it. I've had Tom by my side through all three previous husbands. He started here as a teenager and became invaluable to the family over the years. But what Chelsea is about to say, is the only thing that seems to make some sense. I chose this room to help me stay strong and to face what we might discover. I must put my big girl pants on as dad used to say. Go ahead Chelsea."

"First let me say that I felt Tom's hatred for Paul. It was palpable. Paul and Grandma moving out of here meant his lifelong work would end. I think he wanted to make sure this didn't happen. Whatever it took. Every day Paul spent here, he had mint tea during with lunch and Mojitos in the evening. Suddenly Tom decides to grow mint. He'd bring fresh leaves from the garden just for Paul. Lots and lots of mint leaves. Just before you arrived, I confirmed what I'm about to tell you. Tom uses old pesticides left over from days gone by. They contain arsenic.

CHAPTER TWELVE

"Well now, this adds an interesting twist," Jeff said, as we left the office and stepped out on to the front porch. "I'll call the coroner in Greensville and have them run a test for prolonged arsenic exposure."

"Wouldn't arsenic show up in blood tests?" I asked.

"It could but blood tests show a short-term exposure. We all take in organic arsenic in our lifetime. Like from seafood. But to check for serious and dangerous sustained levels, you need to do hair and fingernail sampling."

"What did you think of Chelsea's theory about Tom being jealous of Paul? Or maybe just afraid of being moved off this estate?"

"I think it's a possibility. One basic human need is a

sense of stability and security. Take that away and it might be reason enough for him feel threatened by Paul."

"Can I go with you?"

"You are thinking the same thing I am?"

"Pay Tom a brief visit in his garden?"

Jeff nodded. "I'd love to have you come with me Jackie. It might make Tom less defensive, soften the interview. I'll approach it as verifying the time Paul left here Friday night."

We found Tom working in his greenhouse.

"Couple of questions for you Tom if you don't mind. You knew Paul pretty well right?" Jeff said.

"Sure, he's been seeing Eleanor for about six months. He used to stay in town, but past three months he got put up at the old place. Wasn't proper for him to stay here at Harmony House."

"But he visited here quite a bit?"

"Yes, he did. Once they started fixing up the old place, he seemed to stay more. Getting acclimated he'd say. Funny word to use. Since I never spent much time in a big city, I didn't know what he meant. But he'd say, he enjoyed the fresh country air, water from your own well, nature's scents."

I stepped in with the next question. "About Saturday night Tom, you mentioned that Paul left here in the afternoon. But someone else spoke of Paul having drinks with Eleanor much later than that."

Tom slowly rubbed his chin before he spoke. "I said it was the last time I saw him. Might not have seen him return is all. My cottage does not have a clear view to the front of the big house."

"Did you notice anyone else here later that evening though?"

"That goofball wanna be mechanic Billy showed up."

"You saw him?" I asked.

"No, but his car has a unique sound, and I heard that."

I asked Jeff. "Isn't that the tow truck driver who showed up to pull Paul's car out Sunday morning? Why would he have come here late on a Saturday night?"

Tom answered my question. "He fancies Chelsea. If you ask me, I think she enjoys the attention a little too much. Maybe leads him on if you know what I mean."

"Thanks Tom. We just needed to clear up that issue. I think you've straightened that out for us," Jeff said.

My gut feeling was to avoid asking Tom directly about the arsenic until testing results came in. I interrupted Jeff's questioning by saying, "You really have some lovely herbs growing here."

I strolled further into Tom's domain, the greenhouse.

"Do you mind if I pinch off a couple of leaves, like

the basil and cilantro? I'm sure my Aunt Ruth would enjoy those. Oh, and maybe some oregano! Goodness you've done quite a job here."

Tom beamed. "Why thank you Jackie. This little piece of the earth brings me so much joy. Please help yourself to whatever you'd like."

I collected a small pile of herbs and Tom handed me a small paper bag to put them in before Jeff said, "Jackie, I've got to get going. Catch you later."

"Bye Jeff, I'm not far behind. There was some information I forgot to give Eleanor so I'm stopping back in the house. Have a good day."

I left the gardens a few minutes after Jeff. Tom's off-the-cuff comments about Chelsea and Billy confused me. Are Chelsea and Tom trying to suggest something nefarious about each other?

Chelsea was on the front porch of the mansion waiting for me.

"Jackie, I wanted to tell you I'm so grateful you're helping Grandma witt. I know she seems strong, but she has her low moments too. I just wanted to catch you and tell you that."

"Thank you, Chelsea. I don't want to seem like I'm interfering, but things keep popping up and your grandmother asked me to help. I forgot to give Eleanor those phone numbers regarding Paul's family. Is she in the house?"

"She is, but why don't you give them to me? I'll get them to her. Maybe just text them to me?"

I collected the information and forwarded it to Chelsea's phone number.

"Got it. Thanks again Jackie. When are you are heading back to Chicago?"

"I was going to leave today but I may postpone it. No big rush. Say Chelsea, I'm a little confused about Saturday night. Paul came back with Alan later in the evening, right? Was anyone else here?"

Chelsea nodded. "No, just them. And I think Grandma said they left around 10:30."

"Ah yes, that's right. And you all just went to bed? Bet it was a restless night with the big day coming up."

Chelsea said, "Sure. Right. Lights out. I wanted her to get some sleep so she could enjoy the ceremony and celebration Sunday. Why do you ask?"

"I'm sorry. Maybe I'm getting too wrapped up in this. Gosh, I wish I wouldn't have promised my Aunt Ruth I'd find out what caused the accident. We'll check out the arsenic that you mentioned. That was a great discovery on your part. Maybe you should be helping Jeff!"

I started down the flagstone path toward my car. "Oh

my, looks like my right front tire is low. Do you see it Chelsea?"

Chelsea walked with me to the car to check it out. "It doesn't look low to me. Do you have a tire gauge?"

"Darn, no. You know I thought I felt it pulling a little on the drive from Chicago. I'd better have it checked out. Do you know of a good mechanic in town? Wait, I'll go to the garage that young man who towed Paul's car works at. Do you know him? He seemed very nice."

"Do you mean Billy? I know him."

"Wait a minute. I'm thinking I heard gossip that he was your boyfriend."

With a derisive laugh Chelsea said, "Small towns! I wouldn't call him my boyfriend. I mean we're really very different people. We hung around together a couple of times. But he was assuming too much, so I was trying to let him down gently."

"That's a sticky situation for sure. When was the last time you saw him?"

"Why do you ask? Did Tom tell you he was here Saturday night? Figures. Yes, I forgot to mention he was here that night. It upset him that I didn't invite him to the wedding. He left in a huff. That's the last time I saw him. I need in and check on Grandma."

"Sure. Please don't forget to give her those phone numbers."

. . .

*T*he jacks holding up the car above Billy's torso appeared unsteady. One leaned haphazardly. I walked closer toward him and cocked my face down to get his attention.

"Billy?"

"Morning ma'am," Billy said from underneath the vehicle. "Hang on. Let me get out." I heard the clang of tools being set down. He pushed himself out on a wheeled dolly. He stood and reached for a red rag from the back pocket of his oily overalls. Wiping the grease off of his hands he said, "What can I help you with?"

"Morning. I'd appreciate you checking my tires. On the ride here from Chicago it seemed like I felt a little pulling on one side."

"No problem."

He tested the air and pronounced my tires perfect.

"You look familiar to me. Were you the tow truck driver at that accident scene yesterday morning? The one where the driver died," I asked.

Billy's radar didn't seem to pick up on the question being odd in any way. "I was. How'd you know that?"

"I was the person who discovered the wreck. Well, myself and my friend Wanda. We were hiking on a trail that left from behind her motel."

"She the lady that owns the Riverview? My aunt is a night manager there. Too bad about that guy. The wreck didn't seem bad enough to kill him. Maybe he had a heart attack or something before he ran off the road."

"Very perceptive. You know that's sort of what I thought too. You might be right about him having some sort of health crisis and passing out before driving off the road. So you didn't notice anything odd on the car?"

"Like what?

"I don't know exactly. I had a friend who was hurt in a car accident caused by a manufacturing defect in the car. The auto industry wants mechanical failures reported I'm sure."

"Nothing I noticed, but then I was just hired to tow it so can't say I was looking for anything. And his car was an expensive one. I'm sure it would have had a recall issued if something was causing problems. From what I heard, the guy was pretty wealthy. I imagined he had the car serviced all the time and checked for warranty issues. I did see some scrapes and scratches. But those could have come from the accident. Me here, I only get to work on older cars. Couldn't afford all those computer things mechanics need now."

"That's got to be tough. I noticed the car was still here last night. You didn't tow it directly to the salvage yard that day?"

"Nope. Old man Cutter didn't want to bother opening up to take it in. Took it there this morning."

"Ah, I see. Well thanks for checking the air in my tires. How much do I owe you?"

Billy waved me off, his fingers forming a zero. He got back on the creeper dolly and pushed himself under the car again.

I leaned down and called out. "Oh Billy, one more thing I was wondering about. You knew a little about the man in the accident. You said word had it he was wealthy."

"Just what I heard. Don't know if it's true or not."

"Did you know he was engaged to Eleanor Harmony who lives in Harmony House?"

"Yes, ma'am I did."

"Did she or anyone come here to take items, personal belongings, out of the car while it was at your shop?"

Billy was quiet. Then, from under the car I heard him answer. "I thought Chief Mathis did that at the scene."

"Oh right."

I decided to take a gamble. "It's just that I thought I saw Eleanor's granddaughter here at the garage last night. I think you know her. Chelsea Harmony?"

Again quiet. Then Billy slowly pushed himself out from under the body of the car, barely missing one of those wobbly looking jacks. "She was looking for some of the guy's stuff she said. So, I let her look in the car. Was I wrong to do that?"

"Oh no not at all. I'm helping Eleanor with some funeral arrangements and she asked me where the car was taken. Did she find anything?"

"I don't know. I gotta get back to work now."

"I'm sorry to keep you. Where was it you took the car?"

Billy lay there looking up at me. "Why?"

"I'd thought I'd have someone there check it for a failure or tampering."

He got off the dolly and moved close to me. "Seriously? Who'd want to tinker around with that old guy's car?"

I took a step back and tried to make my laugh sound natural. "Just a usual question in an accident like this."

"It's at Cutter's Auto Salvage Yard. Want me to get you the address?"

"I can check online," I said.

"Let me write it down for you. I doubt old man Cutter has anything online. He likes to fly under the radar if you know what I mean." Billy left to enter some sort of office through a door marked with layers of smudged fingerprints.

I think I did know what he meant by flying under the radar. I once worked with a reporter writing an exposé on the underground world of chop shops, places that quickly disassemble stolen cars to sell the parts for a profit. I hoped that wasn't what I'd be walking into. Maybe he meant Cutter liked cash, a less dangerous reason to want to stay away from police radar.

Billy returned with a scrap of adding machine tape. An address, printed with a thick pencil, written on it.

"Thank you. Oh, and Billy, one more thing..."

The look he gave me made me change my mind. I didn't need information from a jilted boyfriend or whatever he was to Chelsea. Too easy for people to see things differently based on their emotions. I needed to clear up a couple of other things first. I palmed my forehead and said, "Nothing. Have a good day."

CHAPTER THIRTEEN

*T*he tall chain-link fence surrounding Cutter's Salvage Yard was topped with barbed wire. Entry gates stood wide open. Inside a dog kennel near the entrance, a large Doberman Pinscher. His snarly bark echoed across the rusty bodies of vehicles in various states of dismemberment. I'd never seen a Doberman this big before. A couple in my building had a min-pin, a miniature Doberman Pinscher, quite far removed from this majestic looking animal now lunging at me from the other side of his pen.

The only vehicles that appeared operational were a gritty old Ford van and a small red compact. They were parked by a ramshackle metal shed. A voice inside shouted, "Shut up Spike. Down." Immediately the dog stopped and sat on his haunches, staring at me.

A dirty unshaven man wearing greasy bib overalls appeared in the shed's doorway and walked toward me.

"Mr. Cutter?" I asked through my open car window.

He moved the tooth pick he'd been chewing to one side of his mouth and said, "Who's asking?"

"My aunt lives in Harmony. Her friend's car was towed in here early this morning. My name is Jackie, and I wanted to look at the vehicle."

"Well if that ain't the dumbest request. Watcha got to look for? The insurance will probably total it. Nothing to be done now, unless you wanna buy it for cash."

I eyed up the man, who was a good foot shorter than me. "Mr. Cutter, I'd like to be honest with you if I may."

He snorted. "Now when was the last time I heard that?"

I laughed as a big old grin, which showed a few missing teeth, broke out across his whiskery face.

"No seriously. I'd like to lean on you to tell me anything you notice that could be a mechanical failure on the auto. Perhaps something that could cause an accident."

"Got it. Insurance claim, right? There's always an angle. But I don't think that's your angle. Now tell me, honest like, what is it you want to find?"

"You're right, I have no interest in an insurance claim. I'm just here on behalf of an interested party trying to clear up a few things. Mechanical failure might be one thing. Anything odd that catches your eye, like maybe something was purposely…"

"You asking me to check if someone messed with the car?"

I smiled. "Hm…that's an interesting idea." I reached in my pocket to pull out the bill I'd tucked there in preparation for just this moment. "I mean, you'll be taking the parts out anyway, right? And you're so experienced with automobiles. I'm sure you'd notice if something unusual shows up."

"Well that sounds like a lot of bother."

"…and for your trouble, I'd like to give you this."

He winked at me as I handed him the bill along with my business card.

"I will keep my eyes open. But I have a lot of cars ahead of the one you're interested in."

I pulled a second bill out of my other jean pocket. "I'd appreciate it if you would move it up in the line." He reached for it, but I pulled it back. "Would now work for you?"

"I believe it would," he said taking the money. "The wreck is over this way."

We walked around the backside of the shed and there was Paul's Mercedes. Cutter pointed out the odd scrape that Stuart had picked up in my photograph. "Now the scrape could have come from the accident."

When I pointed out the odd paint color hidden in the metal cuts and under the layer of dirt, he hitched up his bibs and squatted down, peering more closely. "Good eyes Jackie. Odd color. Know of only one guy around here with that color vehicle. Ed Gray."

He walked around the rest of the car, offering no further opinion about the situation until I prompted him to give me his thoughts.

"Nothing jumps out at me. Course I'd have to lift this wreck to check the undercarriage, and the hood is jammed shut. It'll take effort to get it open."

"Look Mr. Cutter, I think I've…"

"Cool down little lady. I'll still do it, just not today. Bright and early tomorrow morning."

As he walked alongside me on my way back to my car, he offered to buy me a can of pop from an ancient vending machine. I've learned in my travels around the world that, when in an unfamiliar environment, it is nice to accept offered hospitality. He handed it to me, pointing to an old splinter filled bench seat. Sitting down I accidentally kicked another can over, the straw in it fell out and pop puddled in the dry dirt.

"Oops, sorry."

Cutter kicked the can under the bench where it joined some empty chip bags, a beer bottle, and assorted trashy remnants.

"Can I speak freely Mr. Cutter?"

He spit on the ground before saying, "Go ahead."

"I knew about the scrape and so do the police. They will question Ed. He might lie about when the scrape happened. Or he might have an alibi."

"He's a boozer. Maybe left the accident so he wouldn't get another DUI. Sick revenge is an ugly mistress."

I was taken aback by this almost poetic line coming from the greasy guy sitting next to me. "Ah yes right. But how did you know about Ed blaming Paul for losing his business?"

"Small town lady. Small town. Now I get a question. Who's the interested party you're nosing around for?"

"Eleanor Harmony."

J'd just gone back out through the gate when Jeff called with the news that after talking to Eleanor and Chelsea, he'd not only asked for hair and fingernail testing from the Greensville coroner, but he'd also made a very interesting visit to Ed Gray.

"I've had a few encounters with the man. He's a hothead. But not such a loudmouth with a Monday morning hangover and a lawman knocking at your door. At first, he hemmed and hawed around, grumbling about needing a morning cup of coffee. I told him it was long past morning but that the station always had fresh brewed coffee on hand, and we could go there to talk. Well that changed his tune pretty darn fast. Didn't take long to have him tell me he was on the back road Saturday night. He saw a weaving car approaching him. He claimed he didn't know who was in the car because the headlights blinded him."

"That's great Jeff. He did sideswipe Paul?" I asked.

"He admitted to it. But he claims the guy just kept driving, so he figured he'd just let him go and wouldn't chase him to make him pay for the damages. It was all I could do to keep from laughing."

"Did he know whose car he hit?"

"He didn't. But I told him. So, then he tells me if he'd known it was Paul Griffin, he would have tried to give the car an extra bump. Tells me those so and so kind of guys deserve it because of what they do to people like him."

"Talk about grudges!"

"Part of me understands the anger directed at hedge

fund managers or private equity firms…heck I don't even know the right word for them. Ed's business was on its last legs and he took a chance. He mishandled things."

"But it's easier to blame someone else. What's next for him?"

"I threatened him with a charge of leaving the scene of an accident. I think the evidence is enough to do that. And he admitted to it. But I don't know how much further I can go with it. There were no evidential tire tracks on that gravel road."

"Do you believe him about seeing the car keep driving away?"

Jeff shook his head. "Here's a bit of news Jackie. I did question him again, and Ed says I should ask the guy who was in the car with Paul. Looked like maybe they were arguing and that was why he was swerving all over the road. Don't blame me because you can't do your job. The old Ed is wide awake at this point."

"Someone else was in the car? Maybe it was Alan?"

"Heck drunk as Ed probably was, he might have seen ten people in the car. I told him I'll try to find that person, but I think he was just trying to figure a way out of this," Jeff said. "What about you? When I left you had something you to needed to tell Eleanor."

"I did, and I learned some things. First, I went to see

Stuart at the paper this morning, to share my accident photographs. He zoomed right in on that scrape on the side of the car. He even picked out the unusual color of paint left behind. And beyond that, Cutter at the salvage yard saw the same thing. Both of them said it had to be Ed."

"Hold on Jackie. What were you doing at the salvage yard?"

"I wanted to see Paul's car again. I'm trying to rule out mechanical failure and tampering. Or like Billy called it, tinkering."

"Billy? Jackie, are you just stirring things up for no reason?"

"Excuse me? I'll have you know that I'm doing this for..."

"I know, for Eleanor. But what beyond Ed Gray side-swiping Paul's Mercedes and Tom using old nursery chemicals, both of which might have been strictly accidental and not meant to harm anyone, led you to talking to Billy and Cutter?"

I was steaming. Who was he to scold me like some off the wall conspiracy nut? I took a deep breath so I wouldn't say anything I regretted. Jeff sensed he pushed the wrong button, so he backpedaled before I spoke.

"Sorry Jackie. I'm just worried about you. I know you're street smart and big city savvy and all that. But just because this is a small town, doesn't mean it's all lollipops and rainbows here. Just be careful."

Now what did that mean?

What things were going on beneath the surface in Harmony?

Not so harmonious?

CHAPTER FOURTEEN

"*D*id you talk with Eleanor today? I asked Ruth when I got back to the studio.

"I tried but just got the answering machine, left a message with the usual *if you need anything give me a call.* She'll probably not suggest anything. I wish I could think of something specific to do. You saw her right? How is she?"

"I feel bad for her. Here they had these plans like fixing up the Mill House to move in to."

"Downsizing makes sense. She has financial means to make choices, but it's not all financial, it's lifestyle. I want to downsize too, to a place like Shady Pines. I'm so glad you're going to see it tonight."

I heard the wistfulness in Ruth's voice. Had I been so wrapped up in my work and myself that I missed how much maintaining the studio and the business was costing her in dollars and mental stress?

"I wonder what will happen to Harmony House now," Ruth said.

"You mean now that Paul's gone?"

"That and just generally. Rumors have swirled for years about the site being used for vacation condos or a resort. Eleanor's been dealing with all sorts of realtors approaching her to buy the property. It would kill her to see the house demolished."

"She's still planning on moving into the old house. I stopped by there today and a crew was working away on remodeling or rehabbing or whatever you call it."

"Did you get to meet Scott there? He's such a handsome man."

"I did. Agreed, he's easy on the eyes. But way too young for you Ruth!"

"First off, not at all. It's a new day in the dating world. I'll have you know that several ladies in town here are panthers," Ruth declared.

"You mean cougars?"

"Whatever. They date younger men."

"A generation younger?" I teased.

She avoided answering by throwing it back at me. "But he's not too young for you. And that man is a hard worker. He and Patti divorced about four years ago.

Seemed amicable enough. In fact, it's their son that my assistant Mandy just married."

"Really? When will they be back from their honeymoon? Wednesday you said?"

"I said that. I also said you could stay another day or two and meet her," Ruth said.

"I'll think about it. But now on to Shady Pines. Why do you like it so much?"

"My lifelong friends live there and that's a big part of the attraction."

I burst out with, "Shady Pines Ma, Shady Pines. What a classic! I remember curling up with you on Saturday night. Us and that big red melamine bowl full of popcorn in front of us. Loved the Golden Girls. Such great casting."

"And the writing. Funniest sitcom I ever watched. Turn here Jackie. Welcome to Shady Pines!"

The Shady Pines Retirement Village was outside of Harmony on the shores of the Wisconsin River. Large white pines stood proudly over a deep blanket of needles covering the ground at their feet. Their clean evergreen scent filled me as we entered the grounds.

"This was built as a Lutheran Church camp in the 1930s. It had not been used for many years. When it came on the market a small group of retired investors bought it. They formed a condominium style of ownership. Any more homes built here have to fit the rustic cabin or cottage style. Everyone pays a monthly fee for landscaping and snow removal."

I heard the wistful tones in her voice. I can see why she would like to settle in here. Gosh, I hope she can make it happen. Maybe Mandy would want to buy the studio. Or some outside interest would see the tourist boom coming to Harmony. The studio's location on Main Street would be desirable. I'm sure it would fetch a good price. I mentally crossed my fingers that one day soon Ruth could move here.

"This is gorgeous! Not at all like I pictured. Can I put up a cottage and live here too?"

"Nope only us old folks. Look, there are my friends."

Three women waved to us from a patio table on the outside of a large log building. That must be the community center I thought. How this placed must have looked when it was filled with young campers.

"Betty, Eunice, Dorothy, meet my niece Jackie."

"Welcome to Shady Pines, Jackie," Dorothy said. "We are having Tom Collins tonight. Ruth, I know you'll have one. Jackie, what about you?"

"I have a vague recollection of what that is. Sour, sweet, and vodka?"

"It's gin dear, but I can make yours with vodka. Or

make it a John Collins with bourbon," Dorothy said with a smile. "We're open to requests."

"I'll do the standard, but light on the gin. I'm driving."

They soon settled me in with a Collins in one hand while reaching for some cheese and crackers from the table in front of me. The conversation swirling around me was focused on Eleanor's canceled wedding.

"We were just shocked to hear about the accident," Betty said. "Here she was marrying for what, the third time and bam, he's gone. Poor dear."

"I think it was the fourth time," Eunice said, munching on a cracker. "She sure kept on finding husbands. Hope she had a prenup. With her family wealth I'm sure she made an attractive package for some gold-digging men."

"Don't be so cynical Eunice," Ruth scolded. "I think Paul really cared for her. And he had his own wealth. Eleanor was obviously devastated, but she pulled it together and had all the food that was being set up for the wedding put out for the guests."

"Guests? She didn't cancel the wedding? For goodness sakes, that's a little sick don't you think," Eunice retorted.

"Jackie only discovered the wreck Sunday morning. There wasn't time to reach everyone and cancel the plans," Ruth said.

"I think it was gracious of her," Betty said. "And brave."

Eunice snorted. "Brave? How brave?"

"Why I'd just curl up in a ball if the man I loved and was going to marry was just suddenly struck dead! I say she was brave to get right out there and face the world again."

"I agree," Ruth said. "It was good to be surrounded by friends and family giving you support in such a rough time."

"You're the person who discovered the car wreck? How did that happen?" Dorothy asked me.

All four pair of eyes spun toward me, except Ruth who was in the middle of a big sip of her Tom Collins.

"My friend Wanda and I set out on a hike up the path from behind her motel. A glint of light among the trees in the hill above us caught Wanda's eye. She thought it was trash and climbed to collect it. But it was Paul's car. It slid or rolled off the road from above and was obscured from sight."

Betty jumped in. "Wanda? That Mathis girl? I love what she did with that old motel! It had been such an eyesore for years and now it's just cute as can be."

I was glad to let the conversation switch from the accident and its aftermath.

Betty continued. "She's set up for all the tourists that

will come to Harmony. Why it's just a perfect location right there on the river."

"Unless that big resort gets put in," Eunice said. "A behemoth place against the little Riverview Motel? Wanda doesn't stand a chance."

Ruth added. "I'm not sure how I feel about it. I love our small town. Been here all my life. But it would mean more jobs for the area and we sure could use that."

"And more taxes collected so maybe they'd fix the potholes on our roads. Or pave that road up the back way on Harmony." Dorothy added, before leaning toward me and asking, "Could you walk to my cottage with me? The way these gals are drinking tonight, I need to make a pitcher of these Collins!"

"Sure, I'd be glad to."

"You know your aunt would love to move here don't you? Duke passed away and his cottage is up for sale. We are all hoping she can buy it."

"It looks like this would be a terrific spot for her. I'd be happy to see her here. It's beautiful."

"Jackie, can I be candid with you?" Dorothy said as she opened the screen door to her own small cottage home.

"Sure."

"Please don't repeat what I'm about to tell about to Ruth."

Dorothy sensed my hesitation. I didn't like keeping secrets.

"I'm asking you for discretion for a good reason. I feel when you hear what I'm about to say you'll understand. May I continue?"

"I suppose so. But I've learned that it's not always best to keep a secret."

With a small nod, Dorothy reached into one of her simple pine cabinets. "I understand what you're feeling, but let me tell you what I want you to know. Your Aunt Ruth would buy Duke's cottage in a heartbeat." Dorothy pulled out a liter bottle of gin and cracked it open. She poured some into the pitcher and added mixer to it.

"So why doesn't she do it?" I asked. "She said she'd like to sell and move here."

"The market for her type of business is dwindling. Her building's location is good, but until more tourists start coming here and bring their money to spend, the location isn't worth what she would need to get. So, she keeps the operation going for now. Plus, the apartment is her home. The girls and I wanted to let you know this because maybe, with your connections, you might be able to help Ruth with her dream of joining us at Shady Pines."

Dorothy pushed the screen door open with her back, holding the pitcher in front of her and I followed her out. "God, I hate that name. Always makes me think of Sophia in the Golden Girls. Shady Pines, Ma. Shady Pines."

"And the character Dorothy said it!" I laughed as I joined her outside.

She rolled her eyes. "Don't I know! I always get told look who ended up at Shady Pines."

"But seriously, I appreciate you telling me about my aunt's situation. I'll see what I can do."

We rejoined the festivity as the sun set on Shady Pines and Harmony Hill and the Wisconsin River.

On our drive back home, I told Ruth how much I loved knowing she had such a great group of friends. "How long have they been living at Shady Pines?"

"Hmm, Dorothy about four years. Betty and Eunice moved in maybe six, seven years ago. I'm so glad you got to meet them. Now this old lady is putting herself to bed."

After the brief conversation I'd had with Dorothy, I knew I needed to better understand Ruth's situation. "Do you have any interested parties in buying your place here so you can move to the Pines with your friends?"

"Not really. That's just a pleasant dream. I like my little apartment here."

Now I knew she was covering up. "Do you think Mandy might buy it from you?"

"I doubt she could afford it. They are just starting out and I know she would love to have children. Unless her father-in-law would give them some upfront funding. But I'm not holding my breath." She gave me a hug and kiss. "Goodnight Jackie."

"Mind if I make some decaf and sit outside a bit?"

"Be sure to grab that throw from the couch. It's dropping into the high forties tonight."

I wanted to think about what Dorothy had told me. Would someone take over the place as a photography studio? Fix it up using Main Street grants? Maybe one of those dress-up in old time clothes and get a photo taken places like Ruth had mentioned? Was that still done? I remember seeing them in tourist places. Maybe with a farm theme, or trappers and outdoor stuff? Oh and old-fashioned photo booths seemed to pick up steam in the past years. If tourism came, a nice photography art gallery might work! I could get friends to display their work.

Ruth was right. I put my coffee down and went back in to get the throw off the couch, aka my bed. Back outside, shadows of trees moving in soft evening breezes cast by lamppost lights. Crickets contributed melodic chirps to this quiet Monday evening. Just a few doors down, jukebox songs carried out to the night air.

Several customers drifted out of Shorty's and walked away into the night.

Letting out a big sigh, I took another sip of my coffee and snuggled my shoulder back under the throw. I noticed lights still on at Billy's garage again tonight. Hard-working young man. Now I wished I'd ask more about his opinion on a potential cause for the accident. I'd hesitated earlier today because of his relationship with Chelsea.

Then I saw it.

Outside the garage.

Amongst the moving gloom created by swaying tree branches.

A shadowy figure slid along the edge of the building and into the deep darkness behind it.

CHAPTER FIFTEEN

*M*ain Street in Harmony was waking to another spring morning. Through the windows of the Harmony Diner where booths were filled with customers. Stuart was unlocking Harmony Hills Happenings newspaper office. Since today's paper was already out, he'd be starting on Friday's edition. At Billy's garage the usually open overhead door remained closed. Across the street Hannah stepped out of Sutton's Antiques and put a signboard on the sidewalk.

I was packing my photography gear back in my car, preparing for my drive back to Chicago this afternoon. But when Hannah waved at me, I decided I'd go over and introduce myself and maybe take a peek inside the building that once held my mother's dress shop.

Hannah was super gracious and showed me around.

Sutton Antiques was lovely. Pieces artfully arranged in clever tableaus tempted prospective buyers. Antique picture frames stacked against a wall caught my eye. "I love these antique frames Hannah. I'll be back next time I'm in town to pick some out. I've seen antique stores in many cities, but yours ranks among the most inviting. The pieces are enticingly displayed," I said.

"Why thank you! I appreciate that. My husband, Mark and I threw caution to the wind and chose to set up a business in an area we both love," Hannah said. "It was fun to hear that your mother used to have her store here."

"She did. The fitting rooms were in the alcove just over there."

Hannah pointed out the front window. "It looks like Ruth is looking for you."

"I'm heading back home today, but I'll be back. Have a nice week."

"Safe travels Jackie, nice to meet you," Hannah said as I stepped out and waved toward Ruth standing on the balcony.

She held the phone up. "Call came in on your mobile, Jackie. But it already went to voice mail. Packing up so soon?"

"Just getting the photo gear loaded up. I'll be right up."

"Okay," Ruth answered.

When I checked the message, I put it on speaker phone so Ruth could hear it too. *Jackie dear, it's Eleanor Harmony. I hope I didn't wake you. I'm coming in to pay my bill at Val's in just a few minutes. Can I stop and see you? Someone told me you planned on leaving today. I have something I must ask you about.*

My first thought was now what is she going to ask me to do? I took a quick mental survey of the things I'd been asked and had gotten done for her. Ruth peered at me over her coffee cup. I could see she was hiding a grin.

"Don't even!" I said.

Ruth turned to fuss with something on the kitchen counter. "Bet she'll ask you for another favor."

"I hope not. Maybe I'll grab lunch with you before I leave town, but that is about it. I actually wanted to talk to Eleanor at some point today though, so now I'll just see her at Val's."

"Sounds good to me. I have a photo sitting scheduled for this morning, so I have to go to work. Lunch it is," Ruth said.

As I sat on the sidewalk bench to wait, I ran through the staging photos I'd taken to show Eleanor. Or maybe I should just send her ones I think she might like? Sometimes I can be so indecisive. It looked like I had over forty. So while I waited for Val's salon to open I began going through them on my tablet and choosing some. So easy with digital to transfer the photos and pull them up on my tablet. That was sure an amazing setting. I could see why a resort would want that prime spot. But they'd take down so many of the beautiful old oaks and sugar maples...which would be a shame.

"Watcha doing there girlfriend?" Val said as she plopped down next to me.

"Just waiting for you missy."

"I haven't seen you since Sunday morning. That was a pretty crazy day."

"It was. Did you hear Eleanor kept all the caterers and musicians and florists there and let them serve food and play music? Like for an Irish wake."

"What's an Irish wake? Have you ever been to one?" Val asked.

"It's where there's food, drink, music, and good company to celebrate the life of the person who died. And yes, I did actually get to attend one. The Irish are a warm and fun group."

"How did it look to see a dead guy? I mean you found Paul, right?" Val grimaced. "In my sixty some years I've never seen a real dead person outside a casket."

"Real dead person as opposed to kind of dead?"

"Smarty pants! You know what I mean. I bet you

have seen bodies, right? Your aunt once showed me photographs you took in a war zone. Was that pretty creepy?"

I flashed back to the exhilaration of combat photography, but also the horrific graphic images I'd captured. "It was creepy...and so very sad."

Val waved circled her hands in the air. "Compared to that..."

"Finding Paul dead in his car was shocking and unexpected, and I knew it would be a sad time for Eleanor, but it wasn't creepy like you say. Right now, in fact Eleanor is on her way to pay her bill from Sunday morning. She asked me to meet her here. So come on girl, let's open this shop up!"

Val pushed herself up from our bench. "Sounds good. And Wanda is my first appointment so maybe we can gab and catch up on your investigation."

"Investigation?"

"I heard you've been checking things out with Police Chief Mathis," Val said in a teasing tone. "That you think this wasn't an accident at all, but a murder!"

"Sorry, no such drama Val." Did I see a disappointed look cross her face?

"But I heard Ed Gray was being arrested for murder," Val said.

"Ed Gray arrested? For murdering Paul?" Wanda said

as she snuck up behind us. "Did I hear you right? Explain how please. He died from crashing his car down a hill. Oh darn, she said, that reminds me I forgot to ask Nadine about that key card Jeff found. But maybe it's no big deal now that Ed's been arrested. You're thinking Paul didn't just fall asleep at the wheel?"

I had to nip this in the bud. "Hold on both of you. I'm not sure he's been arrested. And it would not be for murder, but maybe for leaving the scene of an accident."

"So, smarty, if it's not an investigation what were you doing at the salvage yard yesterday?" Val asked.

"What? How did you hear about that?"

Val snapped a pink plastic cape and wrapped it around Wanda's shoulders. "Just an overheard conversation from the bar last night. I met one of my customer's there for a beer and Cutter was asking Shorty who you were and why were you snooping around his junkyard. I think he's the one telling everyone about Ed Gray being arrested."

At that moment Eleanor and Chelsea walked in. "That's just what we want to talk to you about Jackie."

Val looked shocked. She stuttered, "Oh gosh, I'm sorry you heard that. I didn't mean to be speculating about such a tragic thing."

"Nonsense if something nefarious happened to my Paul I want to hear about it. Chelsea and I have something more to contribute to your investigation too. Don't we?"

Again, with *my investigation* I thought!

Chelsea nodded, turning her eyes down. "We might," she mumbled.

Eleanor reached out and pulled Chelsea in against her. "Poor thing. We got a call last night from Arthur Cutter. He told me you'd ask him to check out Paul's wrecked car Jackie. He said he found one thing you already knew about."

"The scrape from Ed Gray's truck?" I asked.

"You and Jeff think Ed sideswiped him and drove him off the road?" Wanda exclaimed. "That bastard."

"Ed admitted he sideswiped a car on the road late Saturday night, but he didn't run him off the road. That the driver of the car was swerving and then just kept driving," I said.

But Wanda wouldn't let it go. "Of course, he'd say that. Drunk out of his skull and didn't want another DUI."

I asked Eleanor what she wanted to tell us. But it was Chelsea who spoke. "Let me tell her Grandma. Jackie, I'm afraid I may have brought trouble to our home. You remember asking me about Billy and I said how I was trying to brush him off? Well I guess he took his anger to an extreme. I don't know why he would have done this though. For what reason. He blamed Paul for coming into our lives and changing our relationship. Which I swear we never even had!"

She trembled.

"Go on Chelsea, it's okay. I'm sure you never meant this to go so far," Eleanor said.

Chelsea took a strengthening breath and continued. "Last night when Mr. Cutter called, he also told Grandma that he found evidence that someone had tampered with the car. And that he thought the likely person was Billy."

Chelsea brought her hands up to her face to capture a sob that escaped. Or so it sounded like one. A mean thought popped into my brain...*so now she's not blaming arsenic?*

Eleanor continued for her granddaughter who couldn't seem to compose herself. "Arthur told me about yesterday. When Billy towed the wreck out there, he was complaining about that Chelsea girl to him. Saying how he might be in trouble now. Arthur said that Billy's done some shady stuff before. So, he figured he'd better warn us about what he'd discovered."

Here's where Chelsea collected herself and loudly pronounced. "I don't want to believe Billy threatened to do something like that. To hurt my family."

"Chelsea, you think Billy was vindictive enough to hurt Paul to get to you?" I asked.

"He had a mean side. And then Saturday he found out he wasn't welcome at the wedding and he blamed it on Paul. He always mumbled under his breath about my inheritance."

Eleanor seemed surprised about that admission. "Why didn't you mention this before Chelsea?"

"I'm sorry Grandma. I knew it wasn't true. But Billy got the idea I would lose my inheritance if you married Paul. He didn't believe that I only wanted your happiness. He got the idea to tamper with the car. Naming all sorts of things he could do and they'd never find out. I was so scared."

Eleanor stared at Chelsea a moment longer. I noticed slight frown lines on her forehead. What was going through her mind?

She redirected her attention toward me. "So now that you know what we know, I wanted to be sure to catch you before you left town. Arthur sent photos of the tampering evidence he discovered. You've got to let Chief Mathis know about this. He needs to arrest Billy immediately."

"This raises concerns Eleanor. Jeff will want to interview Arthur Cutter and Billy."

"If this is true, he's got to arrest Billy for I don't

know…vehicular homicide, maybe?" Wanda added her two cents.

"I agree. The little bum. To press this poor child so," Val said.

"He could have done it late Saturday night. Remember I told you he came by," Chelsea said hesitantly.

Chelsea suggested Billy came to the house Saturday night because was upset about the wedding. Was Billy angry enough to mess with Paul's car though? It made little sense to me.

A piercing scream broke my thoughts.

CHAPTER SIXTEEN

We all rushed out of the Cut-n-Curl. When I realized the scream came from the direction of Billy's garage, I raced toward it with Wanda, her pink plastic salon cape flapping out behind her.

A woman stood just outside the front door to the station screaming and pointing back into the building. Stuart Walters was the first to get there, and he rushed past her and into the station. Wanda took the woman by her shoulders. "Connie, stop screaming. Tell me what happened?"

The woman doubled over gasping for air. She was hyperventilating and Wanda maneuvered her to a nearby bench to sit down, putting her head between her knees before she passed out. Chelsea ran past me and we both caught sight of Billy's body, crushed under the auto he'd been working on.

Now it was Chelsea's turn to scream. Her's wasn't a long extended one like Connie's, but a broken half scream half wail, an animal like keening.

Stuart kneeled next to Billy. "I've called the police station. It's too late for us to do anything more for this young man."

I wrapped my arm around Chelsea and walked her back outside, where Wanda took over. "Come on honey. Sit here with us." Eleanor was at the scene now too. Wide eyed and frightened like her granddaughter.

I heard the siren. Another dead body in Harmony. Memories of what I'd seen last night came to me. That figure leaving…sneaking away.

Jeff arrived. I took his arm to stop him before he entered the garage.

"Eleanor and Chelsea told me that Arthur Cutter called them last night and said he suspected Billy of tampering with Paul's car. On top of that Jeff, I saw someone sneak away behind the garage last night."

Jeff directed the EMT's to stand down so a potential crime scene could be processed. He asked Stuart to step outside and get the gathering crowd to disburse.

He turned to me. "Jackie, please can you help? Let Eleanor know I need to talk to her as soon as possible.

Then you and I are going to get a statement from Cutter."

"I'll tell her," I said.

Stuart wasn't being very effective in disbursing the crowd, but he was trying. I overheard concerned townspeople...

Crushed under a car.

Poor kid.

What an awful way to die.

Hard worker.

What happened?

Cheap old tools he had.

Jack collapsed.

I found Eleanor comforting Chelsea. "Jeff wants to talk to you as soon as he's done in there. Can you wait here for him?"

Chelsea paled and asked, "Why?"

"He wants to hear exactly what Cutter told your Grandmother last night."

"But what does that have to do with Billy now? Wasn't he crushed by a jack that failed?" Eleanor asked.

Chelsea was pulling her grandmother away. "I want to go home Grandma. Now."

Jeff called me back into the garage to ask, "Can you do some more crime scene shots for me please?"

Numbly, I pulled out my cell phone. I squatted down

to capture the scene including the body before they lifted the car off.

People were leaning against the glass of the overhead door. Shielding their eyes from the morning sun so they could see into the interior. Stuart hadn't gotten the crowd under control, and it was growing. Through the dirty glass I saw Eleanor, using her most authoritative posture, get everyone to step away. But they didn't leave. Just too much here to see. Further down the street I saw Chelsea talking on her cell phone.

An old Chevy squealed to a stop on the street and a middle-aged woman jumped out, pushing her way into the garage.

"Ma'am you can't go in there," Stuart scolded.

"I'm his aunt. Let me see him."

Stu got a nod from Jeff, and the woman knelt down next to the body. "Oh, Billy what have they done?"

Wanda sidled up to me, reminding me that the woman kneeling next to Billy's body was Nadine, her night clerk at the motel. "She's such a sweetheart and a hard worker just like her nephew."

Billy's aunt looked up, her eyes filled with tears that glistened through her anger. "Chief Mathis, I'll tell you right now this wasn't an accident." In a low quiet voice through gritted teeth she said, "When you're done here, I must talk to you."

"Of course. I'll come by later. I'm so sorry you had to see your nephew this way."

Wanda took Nadine's arm and said, "Billy was a good kid."

Nadine swallowed down a sob. "Thank you, Wanda. Please excuse me now." She held her head high as she walked to her car and drove away. Chelsea turned to watch Nadine leave, but she didn't stop talking on her phone.

*A*n hour later Jeff and I were on our way to Nadine's home at Harmony Manor, the mobile home park outside of town.

Now that I had Jeff's full attention, I told him what Eleanor and Chelsea had revealed this morning. "Cutter didn't strike me as a man given to idle gossip and hyperbole," I said. "Do you think there's something to what he told Eleanor and Chelsea?"

"I don't know. Seems pretty far flung for Billy to do something to the guy's car. I mean why?"

"Two possibilities. Because he's mad at someone he thought was his girlfriend. Or because of what Chelsea suggested to us earlier at the salon. Billy thought Paul being in the picture is what ruined their so-called relationship."

"Jackie, I think I need to hear more about what happened when you talked to Billy and Cutter. You might be on to something."

"After you left Eleanor's house yesterday, I made off with some of Tom's mint leaves in case you want to test them for arsenic."

"Clever detective work."

Was that a compliment? "But I also talked to Chelsea and made it appear I needed someone to check out my tires."

"As in maybe Billy?"

"I wanted to know just what their relationship was, and I caught her in a lie. She said no one but Paul and Alan had been at the house late on Saturday. Tom told me Billy had also been there. He knew it because he recognized the sound of his hot rod. So that led me to the garage on the pretext of my tires needing air. And even I noticed the weak and damaged looking jacks he was using. The kid seemed nice, and not nervous with some leading questions I asked."

"And what did you learn?"

"I sensed a shift in him when I asked about anyone retrieving Paul's things from the vehicle."

"What made you do that?"

"When Billy told me he didn't take the car out to the salvage yard until early Monday morning, I remembered seeing someone I thought was might be Chelsea at the garage on Sunday night. So, next question, seeing she lied about Billy being at the house, what would she have been doing at the garage later? He said she came for Paul's stuff. Did you ever find his cellphone?"

Jeff pulled into the mobile home park. "No, I didn't find his phone. Good call Jackie. And I want to hear more about your day, including meeting Cutter. But right now, it'll have to wait."

The mobile home in front of me was as tidy as a pin. An umbrella shaded a small seating area on a modest paver patio. Flowerpots, overflowing with colorful flowers and vines, edged the patio.

Nadine opened the door and motioned for us to enter. I smelled fresh brewed coffee. Jeff and I both accepted a cup from her. Again, more to ingratiate myself and make her feel comfortable. A momentary flashback to accepting the soda from Cutter yesterday left me feeling I was missing something from that scene.

I shifted focus and listened as Nadine launched into what she wanted us to know. Even when her cat jumped on her lap, she wasn't distracted. The bitterness in her voice blossomed as her story poured out.

"My nephew got caught up in a situation involving Chelsea. I just know it. Everyone thinks Billy was crazy in love with Chelsea. But it was her who pursued him.

She had her reasons. I saw Chelsea here at Billy's trailer lots of times. She's guilty of something. I feel it. Billy's death was no accident. They needed someone to take the fall."

"Whoa now Nadine. Slow down. Who is this they you're talking about?" Jeff asked.

Nadine tightened her jaw and clenched her hands. "This isn't easy for me. I don't like to put myself into other people's business. I have a good life. I like my cat, my home, my job, and my community. But when I hear people dissing my Billy and then to see what happened this morning…"

I took her hands in mine, covering them, willing her the strength to speak. "I knew it was her coming sniffing back around. Didn't recognize her at first."

"Who?" I asked.

Nadine hands went limp. She stared out the window, stroking the large tabby cat lying in her lap. "Billy said she was in town stirring things up again. He always came to me for advice. I just know they were pressuring Billy to do something. I could tell by the questions he was asking me. But he didn't deserve to die crushed under a car."

Nadine's intense distress over finding her nephew dead finally cracked her, and she sobbed into her hands.

CHAPTER SEVENTEEN

"Why did you want to leave?" I asked Jeff. "She might have told us more?"

He said, "Yes, maybe so, but right now the shock of losing her nephew is too raw. I can talk to her tomorrow. I'm wondering if the dissing of Billy referred to the same thing Eleanor was talking about. Might Cutter have been spreading rumors like that beyond his telling Eleanor? Could Billy have tampered with Paul's car? I've seen stranger things."

"Do you think the two deaths are connected?"

"Not right now. I'm not making a snap decision. Keeping an open mind."

That was refreshing for me to hear. Maybe I was the one jumping to conclusions? I asked, "But what about me hearing that argument and seeing a figure leaving?"

"I know you're thinking about what you saw, or think you saw late last night. Can you be sure the voices were coming from the garage? Can you identify the person you saw creepy away from the garage as being Chelsea?" Jeff said.

"No, but..."

"But you're leaving town and leaving behind an unfulfilled promise to Eleanor," he said in an over the top dramatic voice.

"Alright already. Enough with the sad sack face!"

But he didn't stop. "You're dropping our investigation like a hot potato leaving me to pick up the pieces. Me, just a small-town cop who hasn't seen the world like you. Me, a local boy, will have to solve this all by myself."

I couldn't help but laugh at his big puppy dog eyes and down-turned mouth. "I see what you mean. But you won't guilt me into staying."

"Just kidding, Jackie," Jeff said. "But I am sorry to see you leave. Be sure to send me the photos from the garage scene this morning. Oh, and the one's from Paul's accident site. Murph took some too, but I'd like to have yours as well. I heard you were visiting Shady Pines last night. Those lucky stiffs getting to live in that beautiful setting."

He must have noticed my amazed look because he

shrugged. "Small town news again! Anyway, is Ruth planning to move out there?"

"First off I don't think they'd like to be called stiffs. Hits too close to home."

Jeff laughed. "Oops!"

"And yes, Ruth would like to live there, but she has a business to try to sell first."

"My cousin Wanda thinks you should take it over. And she makes a good case for it. The town is growing as a tourist destination. A beautiful photographic studio of your work would be a genuine attraction."

"Wanda said all that huh?" I had to smile. She sure was pushing for me to spend more time here. "What do you think about this resort business that's supposedly going help bring in tourists?"

"I'm kind of on the fence about it. And so are half the townspeople. I mean there's lots of land around here to build on. But they seem to have their sights set on Harmony Hill. Least that's what Kim says."

"Kim Walters? Is she involved with that?" I asked.

"Kim is involved with most any real estate deal in this area, especially one that could be as lucrative as this. The Harmony Griffin wedding and their move to the old place would be the final step so she could put together a deal."

"So that might have changed with Paul's death?"

"I'm not sure Jackie. Small town rumors fly around like crazy. Scott might know more. You know I had a question for Scott anyway since he's working at the old place. Want to come with me to see him?"

"Sure. I wouldn't mind seeing Scott again. I mean before I leave for Chicago."

I glanced at Jeff and saw the corners of mouth turned up.

"Ah, so you noticed Mr. Drake in a special way did you?"

"Haha."

*K*im Walters and Scott Drake were standing at the lowered back gate of his pickup truck with plans spread out in front of them. They both turned to wave as we pulled in.

Scott and Jeff excused themselves to talk in private and I found myself left alone with Kim. I decided to pick her brain about her vision of the future for Harmony and the hills surrounding it. After all, according to Jeff she was involved with the people who wanted a sizeable chunk of property in Harmony. "Hey Kim, nice to see you again. What are all these drawings? Plans for this Mill House?"

"Goodness no. These are plat maps for our county.

Scott and I were just discussing a contingency plan if the deal for Harmony House falls through."

"What deal was that?" I asked in my most innocent voice.

"Winston Partners had all the paperwork ready to sign based on months of discussion with Eleanor. Then in just the past weeks she sprung it on us that she was planning on pulling out of the deal."

"So basically, it was a done deal with Winston Partners? I heard a different name. Something with Ridgeline in it."

"It's very complicated. Even I, with my knowledge of the business, I am losing track of which one is which. It's like that game with the nut hidden under a shell. Shuffle...shuffle...shuffle! Which one is the buyer under?" Her laugh tinkled in the air.

Shell game, that's exactly what the gals at the Pines had called it I thought. "So did you locate some optional areas for development?"

"I've been piecing some properties together that might work. One of them being the old Harmony Mill site. It's down lower and that means less dramatic views but closer to the river where the boating is."

Kim leaned over, carefully protecting her navy dress from the grit on Scott's truck, as she pointed to an area on the surveyors document spread out in front of us. "If you could pull in this part of the mill property, where one of Eleanor's husbands had started a pallet company, you'd have land to build on at a higher elevation. Maybe create more single cottages on some cute curvy walking paths. But I'm also trying to link these two other parcels, the salvage yard, and this forty-acre farmed parcel. With those two added, direct river access would be a bonus."

"That sounds like a nice idea. Where is the old mill from here?"

Kim pointed further up the side of the hill. "It's abandoned now, but the pallets and old buildings were left behind. There would be some cleanup, because the pallets have been tainting the ground water with arsenic from their coatings. Still it will take a lot of convincing. The purchasers are losing interest with all the delays."

"I thought Eleanor was still planning on moving out of the mansion." I hoped I could elicit a reaction from Kim.

Kim's eyes lit up. She did a quick happy clapping. "That would be amazing. I'm so excited. I'll have to let Alan know that the possibility of buying Harmony Hill and the house is still in play."

"Alan? Why?"

"He's part of Winston Partners. Didn't you know?"

"But I thought his coming to the wedding was because of his past business association with Paul."

Kim shrugged. "These wheelers and dealers have lots of so-called partners. He was super disappointed when Paul wouldn't help him close the deal. Like I mean really upset. Lately Paul has been trying to convince Eleanor to donate the property to the village as some sort of retreat or learning center."

"I knew Paul was a philanthropist from his dealings in the Chicago charity scene. I suppose he'd want to see such a historic home saved."

Kim said, "Sure, no skin off his nose."

The guys came walking back. Kim added, "Thanks for the info on Eleanor. I thought it was too soon to broach the subject, but strike while the iron's hot. Toot-a-loo."

Scott said, "Sorry we dashed off Jackie. Jeff here just told me that my new daughter-in-law works for your aunt. I didn't put that together before. She's a good kid."

"I was hoping to meet Mandy, but Ruth said she wasn't returning until tomorrow."

"Change of plans. My son had a bad allergic reaction to Libby, and they returned early. You might get to meet her after all. She's a great gal and I'm so happy to have her in our family."

"Congratulations man! I didn't know Matt got married. But who's this Libby?" Jeff asked.

Scott chuckled and shook his head. "Sorry, that sounded odd. Libby is Mandy's new dog. Cutest darn thing, but it's looking like one of them, Libby or Matt is going to have to go."

"And I think we know who Mandy will pick. If Libby's so cute I'm sure she'll find a suitable home for her," I said optimistically. "Hope to meet her before I leave."

Jeff put his arm across Scott's shoulder. "This lady here in front of us has been revealing her investigative chops to me. I'm trying to convince her to stay and at least keep taking crime scene photos for me."

"So you're in the family photography business too?" Scott asked.

Jeff stepped back to look at Scott. "Man, she's a big-time pro."

Scott grinned at me with that disarming smile. "Well now, I may not have known of your career, but I'll bet you Mandy will know of you. I'll let her know you'll be at your aunt's place later if that's okay with you Jackie?"

"Perfect," I said.

"As to you Jeff, I can see why you'd appreciate having such a talented and classy looking lady working with you. But what may I ask are the crimes you two have been investigating? To my knowledge, Harmony is a pretty quiet kind of place. Someone stealing old man Schuster's chickens again?"

I burst out laughing. "Hey, I focused my lens down tight on those fox tracks! Seriously though Scott, we've been working on the possibility that Paul Griffin's death, might not have been a simple auto accident."

"Jeff, would your questions about possible arsenic contamination here tie in with it in any way?" Scott asked.

It surprised me Jeff hadn't included me in that conversation. But to be fair, as far as he knew I was leaving town in a few hours. That is if my perpetual curiosity about things would let me. Plus now, I'd like to stay to meet Mandy. Guess there was no harm in staying one more night. I'd been thinking about Ruth's situation and it would be good to get more information from her about that too.

"You've gotten the toxicology report in Jeff?" I asked.

"I didn't want you to accuse me of putting temptations to stay in your path, but yes I got the autopsy and the toxicological reports."

"Come on Jeff, let me see them!"

"And?" Jeff said.

"Okay, you two. I'm up for another evening here in Harmony. I look forward to meeting your new daughter-in-law Scott. And Police Chief Mathis, may I make a formal and respectful request to please see the paperwork you received from the coroner?"

Jeff hoisted his broad shoulders up and hooked his thumbs through his duty belt. "You sure Jackie? I mean this is serious business. The case might take weeks to solve."

CHAPTER EIGHTEEN

*a*s we left the Mill House, Jeff pulled a manila envelope from his records case. "How about we look at these over lunch?"

"You haven't looked at the report yet?"

"Nope I haven't. Just came in this morning and between Billy's death and talking to Nadine I haven't exactly had a lot of time."

"So, these might show nothing to investigate is that right?" I asked. "Jeffery you tricked me, didn't you?"

"I said I didn't see them. But Murph did, and he's the one that alerted me to the amount of long-term exposure to arsenic that the results showed. That's why I wanted to confirm with Scott that the original well was still being used. I know enough about ground water contamination to know it's possible Paul's high level of the poison came from the water he was drinking."

"Kim mentioned it as well," I said. "Said there might be a big cleanup involved if a resort developer bought the property. Chelsea's questioning the arsenic that Paul's doctor picked up on wasn't coming from Tom's mint leaves?"

"Doesn't rule Tom out," Jeff said. "But I'm unsure if I'll bother with testing the mint leaf you snuck out of Tom's garden."

With a bemused smile at Jeff, I said, "I agree. But maybe we should present the option to Eleanor to decide. I mean if Tom was purposely causing harm to Paul, she'd want to know."

"You're right. I'll be taking the autopsy report to her later today. But where does that leave us? Neither the blood test nor the hair test showed enough arsenic to kill him."

"But enough dizziness and confusion to have caused the accident?"

"Possibly," Jeff said as he pulled up to the diner. "Could you get us a seat? I have a quick phone call to make."

I reached for the manila envelope, but Jeff quickly snatched it away. "Hold on, my call involves something Murph saw in the report. I need it with me."

.   .   .

*J*nside the diner I grabbed today's edition of the Harmony Hills Happenings paper. On the front page was my photo of the accident scene along with the caption *Harmony mourns for Paul Griffin, fiancé of Eleanor Harmony, who tragically died in this vehicle accident Saturday evening.* The article explained how, in community spirit, Eleanor didn't cancel the wedding celebration but rather spent the afternoon receiving condolences from her friends and family and treating it as a memorial to her lost love.

It was obvious Stuart had done some research on Paul. He listed companies Paul had been a part of. Stuart wrote, *though by all accounts the cause of death appears to be accidental, if anyone in the area has any information regarding it, please contact Stuart Walters or Chief of Police Jeffery Mathis.* So that's where the gossip about murder might have come from, I thought.

"Thanks for waiting for me," Jeff said as he approached my table, coffee in hand.

"Now how do you rate getting you own coffee? And even a special mug."

"I get to refill this free courtesy of an appreciative local friend." He winked at Dolly who'd arrived with my coffee.

"Gotta love a man in uniform," she said. "You two ready to order?"

Soon as we'd given our orders, I said, "I was just thinking about you."

"I like the sound of that. What may I ask were you daydreaming about?"

"Not daydreaming, thinking." I spun the newspaper to face him and tapped my index finger on the last sentence of the article about the accident.

"You thought of me when you were reading about Joe and Ginnie's wedding? I'm flattered."

"No! This sentence," I said, pointing just above the wedding announcement. "Asking the public for information on the accident. Did you ask Stuart to put that in?"

Jeff took a seat on the booth bench across from me. "He asked me if he could put it in. He's a good guy so I don't mind if he can dig something up."

"I took my photos to his office yesterday. He said he'd been an investigative reporter before, so he might live vicariously through you."

Jeff chuckled. "I don't have investigations of any great depth here...things are usually pretty simple and straight forward. But yes, he told me what he had pointed out to you, about the color of paint in the sideswipe damage and I agreed that must have been Ed's truck. That's why Ed's a person of interest."

"Did you notice the firms Paul partnered in or ran?"

"Quite a list."

"When we were at the Mill House, Kim showed me a plat map. She's working on the sale of property for a possible resort or vacation condo site. She mentioned these two companies."

"I don't know all about that. Or care, I guess. I'm more interested in you seeing this autopsy report. I think you'll be surprised. I know I was."

It didn't take me long to discover the cause of Paul Griffin's death.

Asphyxiation.

I couldn't believe my eyes.

What did this mean? I felt my jaw dropping. I read and reread the words. "He couldn't breathe? Signs of possible manual strangulation? What are they saying Jeff?"

"That's what I asked the coroner. I needed clarification on the medical jargon in this report. The way he sees it is that once the accident was over, the victim was still alive. Might have been passed out. They can't say conclusively. But it appears that the accident didn't take his life. Someone strangled or suffocated him."

"That's crazy."

My mind raced.

"Who would have known he was in an accident? Ed might have! He admitted to sideswiping him. Maybe he saw the car go over the edge and he went to check on him. Found him still alive and in a drunken rage strangled him? No one would know. Late at night. No cars to drive by and see it?"

Jeff shook his head and pinched his lips. "Nope. Murph checked out a trail camera Ed has near his driveway. It proves he came in at eleven and he didn't leave again that night. I drove from Eleanor's to the motel on the same route as Alan and Paul and it took me twenty-five minutes to get to Riverview."

"We didn't find the wreck until eight on Sunday morning. Could he have snuck back out?"

"True, I guess. But I called Alan to talk to him again with this recent information. He confirmed that someone had sideswiped them on the dark road, but that Paul's Mercedes handled it well and they drove on because the guy seemed to swerve and kept going up in the opposite direction. We didn't want want to get into trouble over some auto body work was his exact quote. Alan said that Paul dropped him off at the motel at just before eleven which fits."

"Whoa, this changes things. You believe Alan?" I asked. "I suspect he was involved in the land deals that Paul nixed just recently. I remembered that I found the passenger door open. Did that door get opened by someone who'd been in the car with Paul when the accident occurred? Or did someone open it to get in and murder Paul while he was trapped in a wreck?"

I was still trying to absorb the facts as the autopsy presented them. Someone either was in the car when the crash happened, which doesn't appear to be the case, or someone came across it afterward.

"Now that the story from Alan confirms what Ed told you, maybe you should talk to Stuart. He found out that Alan and Paul had a business relationship in addition to their friendship. And to Stu's wife Kim too. Of all of us, she's probably the one with the most contact with Alan. I have a few things I want to check out myself."

"Can you let me in on your thoughts Jackie?"

"How about we get together and take this autopsy report to Eleanor later this afternoon?" I said.

With *what are you up to look* on his face, Jeff said, "Are you being evasive with me Ms. Parker? I'll let it ride for now, but…"

I appreciated Jeff not pressing me about sharing my thoughts right at this moment. I needed to clear them up in my own head. Things were swirling around me and I wanted to find the threads and weave them together into whole cloth. Speaking about it too soon might sound like speculation.

"Thanks, I'll talk to you later Jeff."

CHAPTER NINETEEN

I left the diner. A good brisk walk always helped clear my head. As a photographer I often have to take my emotions out of the situation. Detach myself from it. And that's what I wanted to do now. Maybe I'd chat with Ruth. Bounce some things off of her.

I circled my fingers to create a pinhole focus that helped me see the Parker Photography Studio store front as I approached it, not as it was during my childhood, but as it is now. Cracks in walls through the new paint job. Warping of the wooden window frames. Rust in the balcony's underside.

It was an old, worn down building, but its bones were good. Great in fact. The scale of the trim work was perfect. The unique upper balcony. With money and patience, we could bring her back to her original beauty. Strip away the layers of paint. Clean up the foundation.

Maybe Kim could find a buyer for it and Ruth would make enough to fulfill her dream of buying a small place in Shady Pines. I decided I'd figure out a way to contribute to that endeavor without hurting her pride. I doubted she'd take a straight cash gift from me, though I'd gladly give it. I'll have to consider what I might do.

A development for tourists would bring in more business for the town's small shops on Main Street. Parker Photograph had a prime location. So does Sutton Antiques. Harmony Diner would see more business than ever. What about the Riverview Motel? I bet Wanda would say competition is good for business. But during the height of the season, this quiet Main Street would be full of cars coming and going. It's really the only main road through the area with all these hills we have here. I don't think there's a straight road in the whole county.

When I entered the studio, Ruth was chatting with a striking young woman. Her brown hair glistened with that pure, untouched by hair color, look to it. She sat on a stool, her feet tucked up on the rung, and her chin cupped in her hands leaning on the front counter. The cutest dog, curling up at her feet, cocked its head at me.

"There you are!" Ruth exclaimed. "Jackie, meet Mandy Drake."

Mandy grinned as she extracted herself from the stool and walked toward me extending her hand. "I'm still getting used to hearing my new last name and I'm loving it."

She was almost as tall as me. A healthy glow spoke of time spent outdoors and her ease of movement spoke of confidence. I liked her already.

"I'm thrilled to meet you. Your aunt has shared much of your creative work with me and it's very impressive. I admit I googled you. You've had quite an illustrious career."

"Thanks Mandy. I'm lucky to have had Ruth's tutelage growing up. And I'm so happy we are getting to meet. Who is this cutie?" I asked, bending down to pet her dog.

"This is Libby." Mandy rubbed Libby's head. "I've been pressuring your kind, gracious, wonderful, welcoming, loving Aunt Ruth to keep Libby for me."

I grinned at Ruth. "She's all of that!"

"My husband's recent allergic reaction to her means I can't keep her at home. I've only had Libby a few weeks and I've had Matt three years so..." Libby rose and leaned against Mandy's leg.

I squatted down and called Libby over. She wiggled

her way over for more cuddles from me. "What breed is she?"

"Shelter dog, so I'm not sure. But she doesn't shed. Rarely barks. Can I name more wonderful qualities for you Ruth?" Mandy clasped her hands together, pleading for Ruth to agree.

I don't remember Ruth ever having a dog, but maybe this was the day. She was wavering.

"I'll keep her here for now. We'll see what happens." Ruth turned toward me. "You seem distracted Jackie. What's going on?"

"I'd planned on leaving today, but I may stay another night, if that's okay with you Ruth."

"Of course, it is. I'm happy you'll get to visit with Mandy then too. Get to know her. She's been such a big help to me."

Mandy asked me about my work and the traveling it involved. I spoke about some of the places I'd been and what my job there entailed. "And I still do the occasional wedding," I said, winking at Ruth. "By the way Ruth, do you do your own framing anymore? I remember Dad used to handle that."

"He was so skilled! Picking out just the right mat and frame material. Sizing it perfectly. We tried some other framers after your dad passed away but, honestly, it was just too much bother. There are so many readymade frames on the market.

"That's one thing I'd hope you think about reintroducing here. I've been taking some online classes on it," Mandy said. "I think there might be enough of a market for it. You can't get a custom frame done except in big craft stores in Madison or Milwaukee. We could stock framing material and I can customize the mats."

"I think you should consider that Ruth. Mandy might be on to something. I asked about it because I'd like to frame several of the photographs I took at Eleanor's on Saturday."

"Why on earth would you want to do that?" Ruth asked.

"Because they are lovely shots of the grounds that were prepped for the big day. And some beautiful inside shots that she might enjoy if she's moving out to the old house. Would you be able to help with that?" I asked Mandy.

"Work with the world-famous Jacqueline Parker. Are you kidding me? I'd love to do that," Mandy said. "Even if it is to just print copies for her."

We discussed how to transfer the photos and Mandy showed me the current editing systems she was encouraging Ruth to get. "The system here needs substantial updating. I'm hoping Ruth will let me do more social media and promotion, too."

As I leaned over Mandy's shoulder and she showed me some of her plans, I found myself lost in the world of photography. This gal's a sharp cookie. She explained about her two-year degree in business management and accounting, and how it would help transition Parker Photography into modern times.

We transferred the digital files and Ruth peeked over Mandy's other shoulder and said, "You know this is a good idea. Eleanor will love these, in a bittersweet way because of what followed, but still…"

This was the first time I'd looked at these photos outside of my camera. I was helping Mandy with some cropping ideas. But the issues with Paul's death, now murder, kept interjecting themselves. I'd decided Mandy had the eye to make the right choices here and that I could get some other things done when something caught my eye.

"Stop, can you pull back out?" There was a small group of people slightly hidden by foliage. I could picture exactly where I'd stood when I took this, but I don't remember anyone being in the shot. They must have been so deep into the shadows.

I pointed to the group and asked Mandy to zoom in tight. It looked to be three, possibly four people. They were in a shady spot and partially obscured. One seemed to be pointing at something, directing the others attention in that direction.

"Do you recognize these people?" I asked.

Ruth tapped the screen. "This one looks like Kim the realtor. She dresses to catch attention and that vivid green dress is unmistakably her style. But I don't recognize that one, except to say it's a woman graced with a lovely set of girls...or the money to buy them. And that one looks like Chelsea."

The fourth figure seemed to be a man, but none of us recognized him from this distance.

"Maybe the woman is with the company buying the grounds for development?" Ruth said.

"Could be," I replied.

"Especially with Kim there. I'm confused about things. The girls at Shady Pines have been researching it and can't seem to pin down who it is who is trying to buy the Harmony Hill property. They mentioned Ridgeline Resorts, or some investment group fronting it."

"I saw Kim earlier today. She's preparing contingency plans in case the original deal falls apart now. In fact, she was at the old house talking to your father-in-law Mandy. But right now, I'll leave editing and printing these to you Mandy. I have a couple of things to take care of."

Ruth asked, "Are you going up to Eleanor's?"

"Not just yet."

With a glint in her eye, Ruth said, "You're up to something Jacqueline. Come on, give us a hint."

After what I'd just seen in the photo, I made a quick decision to trust Ruth and Mandy to keep a secret for the day. "Please keep this under your hat for now. But Paul didn't die in a car accident. He was suffocated."

CHAPTER TWENTY

I needed to talk to Val more about what she'd heard at Shorty's Tavern last night. We'd been interrupted when Eleanor and Chelsea arrived, then of course totally distracted by the discovery of Billy's body.

Val was more than willing to fill me in. "You know, with everything that's gone on now, I have to think he wanted to be heard. Know what I mean? Kind of drawing attention to himself. It was Monday night and only about eight customers in the place besides me and my friend."

"Was Cutter alone?"

"At first, but then some lady came in and sat down near Cutter and started talking to him. He couldn't take his eyes off her cleavage."

"Did you recognize her?"

"Nah. She had a quick drink and left before him."

"What time was that?"

"Cutter was still there when we left," Val said.

"No, I mean her. What time did the woman leave?"

"About 9:30."

$\mathcal{N}$ext I walked to the Harmony Hills Happenings office, hoping I'd find Stuart in. But luck wasn't with me. I got my car. Another person I needed to see was Wanda.

Walking by the diner I saw Stuart inside enjoying an afternoon coffee and pie. I knocked on the window and he waved me in to join him. He welcomed my questions about what he'd printed in this morning's paper.

"You know Jackie, my wife Kim is a realtor and is trying to help with the deal for buying Harmony House. But it's gotten so mixed up. My research into the firms Paul was with at different times caught her eye."

"She told me a bit about it this morning."

Stuart looked surprised when I said that. He quickly asked, "Where did you run into her?"

Before I realized I might be creating a problem, I told him the truth, that she was at the site of the remodeling of the Mill House.

The tone in Stuart's voice shifted markedly as he asked, "Was Scott there?"

"He was."

I could see Stuart's eyes cloud over.

"I'm sorry. Is there something wrong?"

"Nothing to worry you Jackie. It's just that when she left the house this morning, she looked so beautiful, and I told her so. But she knows it. I guess I just look at someone so strong and handsome like Scott Drake and I look at myself and have to wonder what she sees in me."

He let out a sad sigh. "But that's none of your concern. I imagine she said she was asking his advice about other sites. Her deal with Eleanor fell through so she's scrambling. She was counting on a big commission."

"She's a driven agent. It's a cutthroat business."

Stuart gave a distracted nod. "She'd been sidling up to that Alan guy too. They met Saturday at Harmony House. She was hoping to talk to him more after the ceremony on Sunday, but then everything fell apart and he left town."

"Do you mean Alan Morris, Paul's friend who came in for the wedding? She knew him?"

"I can't vouch for the last name, but sounds like it might be the same guy. She took trips to Chicago to meet with some developers and they met there. She was excited to show him around the estate herself. Impress him with her plans."

Alan was the unidentified man in the photograph. Now, who was the other woman? Another prospective buyer or financier?

*J*eff called to see if I was ready to go with him to Eleanor's. I decided to make a quick change of plans and catch up with Wanda later.

"Busy afternoon?" Jeff asked as soon as I slid in his cruiser.

"You might say that. How about you?"

"I did manage to get a couple of things done. Want to hear about them?"

"Sure."

"First off I went back to see my cousin Wanda at the Riverview Motel. We went through her security video. It confirms Alan's story. You can see Alan letting himself into his cottage and what appears to be Paul's Mercedes drive off. He went on up that same back road because he was heading home to the Mill House."

"Could Alan have left again later?"

"I suppose it's possible, but we fast forwarded

through until midnight and didn't see him leave. A couple other guests came and went but not Alan."

"Good call to check that out. I was going to do the same thing."

"The second big discovery came after I called Chelsea to ask if she ever located Paul's cell phone. She said she never found it. Then I contacted Paul's secretary in Chicago. He still has maintained an office there. Thought I'd take a chance and see if she'd do a limited print out of his cell phone calls. It would have been a pain to subpoena them from his cellular provider. But I think my small-town charm convinced her I would be discreet with the information."

"What made you ask for those?"

"The autopsy report. I know you felt it too. Things were feeling a little hinky before then, but knowing he died from asphyxiation things kicked into high gear. He might have crashed and called someone for help. But that someone could have been the one who did him in."

"What do the records show?"

"That Paul made a call at 11:04." Jeff pulled into Eleanor's drive. "And it was to the number of the phone in this house."

CHAPTER TWENTY-ONE

*E*leanor opened the door even before we knocked. As soon as she let us into the house I asked, "Home alone today Eleanor?"

"Tom is outside gardening. It's the maid's day off."

"Is Chelsea here?"

"I don't believe so. She left earlier today, shortly after I told her you were coming. Said she needed some alone time after the tragedy this morning. Poor thing. The shock of losing Paul and then her friend Billy being killed in such a horrific accident. This is probably harder on her than anyone else."

"Except you I'm sure," Jeff said empathically.

Eleanor nodded. "Of course, you know what I mean. She's so young and has had such heartache in her young life. I've always wanted to protect her from more hurt, but here we are. Why do you ask?"

"We wanted to share the autopsy with both of you. It's rather disturbing, and we'd hoped someone would be here by your side."

"I'll be okay."

Jeff said, "A couple of questions first if I may? Did you feel you got all of Paul's records and items from the house and his car? At least as far as you know."

"Yes, as far as I know. Alan is helping with the business end of things and he didn't imply he was missing anything. Chelsea brought a few personal things to me. And the coroner has a package he's sending along with Paul's body to the family. His watch and his wallet I believe. Since I'm not family, I didn't make a fuss over it. What was I to do with any of it? Chelsea said there are still clothes at the house which she plans on donating to Goodwill."

"But you never got his cell phone?"

"I thought Chelsea mentioned getting it out of the car. But I can't be sure of that. Would you like me to ask her about it?"

Jeff said that wasn't necessary at the moment, but I noticed he didn't say he'd already asked her about it. At this point we had the phone records, and that was the most important thing. Instead he said, "Do you have the code to open the phone if we should locate it?"

"I don't."

Eleanor walked us into her father's office to talk. She shut the door behind us. I notice photographs lying next to the printer. I did my best casual walk by and noticed they must have been the ones sent from Cutter last night.

"Anything else I can answer before you show me the autopsy report?" Eleanor asked.

I pointed to the photos and said, "May I?"

"Of course. Jackie, I know I've imposed on your kindness, but perhaps you can get them to someone who could authenticate the tampering damage Arthur Cutter alleged. I appreciated him going through the effort, but I am certainly no judge of that sort of thing. And if it was a mechanical failure, I believe that Mercedes-Benz should be notified."

Why hadn't Cutter called me back? Instead he went to Eleanor and Chelsea with his findings. And then pointed a finger at Billy. Odd.

I quickly handed the photos over to Jeff hoping he caught my *don't you dare pass these back to me* look. "I'll let the police handle that."

"If these photos make tampering look like a cause of

the accident, I'll go to the salvage yard right from here," Jeff said.

"Oh dear, I gave Arthur the go-ahead to break the car down for parts this morning. He assured me the photos would verify that someone had tampered with the car. May I see the autopsy now please?"

Jeff shifted awkwardly. "Just one more thing if I may. I'm sorry to bring this all up now, but we need to discover exactly what happened Saturday night. You understand?"

"You're starting to frighten me. You have these photos showing someone wanted to cause an accident with Paul in the car. What else can you question me about?"

"Did you speak to Paul after he and Alan left the house at 10:30 on Saturday? Or do you know of anyone who did?"

I was glad Jeff didn't mention Paul's phone records showing a call was placed to this house. Unless Eleanor took it herself, it would only raise alarms.

"No, I didn't. He was going to take Alan to the motel and then head right to Mill House to get some sleep." Her voice quivered. "Only he didn't make it."

"You brought the information about the arsenic to our attention. What are your thoughts about that?"

Eleanor brushed Jeff's question aside. "I simply don't

believe Tom would do something like that. I got caught up in all of Chelsea's drama over the possibility of him having some in his system. His doctor couldn't speak to me about a patient without prior authorization. Nonsense I said, before I slammed the phone down. Not one of my prouder moments. Are you still questioning Edward Gray as well?"

"His story checks out. He had a little skid into Paul, but that's all. Alan confirmed it happened that way too."

I felt this might be a time to assure Eleanor that Tom was innocent. "You are right to doubt the idea that Tom had anything to do with poisoning Paul. He had a rather high level of arsenic in his system, but not enough to kill him. And it wasn't from anything here at Harmony House. The stacks of rotting pallets up the hill contaminated the well at the old place with arsenic. Many years it leached into the soil and groundwater, contaminating the well."

"Oh no! I feel awful," Eleanor said, bending her head into her hands and shaking it side to side.

"Please don't trouble yourself. It didn't cause his death," I said, reaching to touch her hand.

Eleanor sat back upright and looked us in the eye. "But it might have caused him to get dizzy or disoriented and run off the road, causing the crash and his death?"

"No ma'm. There's one more factor in the autopsy," Jeff said.

I felt so bad for Eleanor, knowing what Jeff was about to tell her would turn her world upside down.

Her entire body crumbled as she learned someone had murdered Paul.

I said, "Can we get Tom to come and sit with you?"

"Yes please. I need a friend right now to hold my hand."

While Jeff went to find Tom, I asked Eleanor about how Chelsea was taking this. "You mentioned she was very upset. I noticed that same thing Sunday morning when we told you about the accident. Was she happy about you getting married?"

Eleanor's eyes carried such sadness in them. "I think she was torn to be honest. It's been just her and me for most of her life. Did you know her mother abandoned her? What mother does that? There were a few brief contacts over the years. Melody even contacted me once or twice when she got in financial trouble. I stopped sending her money after a while and cut off communication. But it tore up Chelsea. I know she made some bad choices as a teenager, but she's been doing much better these last few years. We've been discussing her future because Paul and I were planning on moving into the Mill House. I know it worried her."

"That had to have been hard for you to be in the middle of. Will you be staying here with Chelsea now?"

"I've decided to still downsize and move to the Mill House. From what I heard today I must be sure to get water from a different source."

"And will Chelsea move there with you?"

"We'll have to talk about it. Paul had a most wonderful idea for Harmony House. Instead of selling this place and the property to the development company as we'd planned, he suggested we donate it to the village for a nature center, historical museum, or some such thing."

"That would be wonderful. I have memories of coming here as a child and seeing the animals and flowers. It was such a treat."

"Thank you for letting me know that. I think it would be a wonderful way to honor my family's memory."

Tom came pushing through the door and hurried toward Eleanor wrapping his arms around her.

CHAPTER TWENTY-TWO

"Well now, what do we do with that phone call thing? A call to this house came from Paul's phone at 11:04. Someone answered it," Jeff said as we drove away.

"Maybe Chelsea forgot about it? Or might Tom have been in the house to answer it? That was the last call made on his phone?"

Jeff nodded. "I'd bet money it was Chelsea he talked to. Why did she lie about it? Kids nowadays. They see the number calling and just don't pick up if they don't want to talk. We didn't have that luxury."

"Or block calls. Our mothers would have yelled out *so and so is calling for you.* We could not have hid."

"With cell phones now you can't hide either. Everyone has one."

"Yep, dating is a whole new game nowadays. Stuff you and I wouldn't even have imagined."

I chuckled at that comment. "You're right. We're not over the hill just yet, but it is hard to relate to how young people see things. We're young baby boomers, I can't imagine what my parents would make of kids dating in this world."

"What is the Billy and Chelsea generation called?" Jeff asked.

"Good question. Are they in their early 30s? I guess they'd be Gen X?"

Jeff shook his head. "So, who are Millennials then? Whatever, it's one thing I don't need to concern myself with. Right now, I need to meet an insurance agent at the station regarding the car jack collapsing. Want me to drop you at the studio?"

"Sure."

"Oh, and did you grab those Cutter photos? I'd like to compare them to the ones you sent over from the night of the accident."

I pulled them out of my leather bag saying, "Great idea. I've got a feeling the comparison will provide some evidence."

"Really? Why?"

"Just a hunch."

Soon as I opened the door to the studio, I caught

Ruth's eye roll and an expression that said I might want to turn right back around.

I was a second too late.

"Jackie! You're just the person I wanted to see," Kim Walters exclaimed. There she stood in her red heels and navy dress with red piping accents. I imagined her standing in front of the mirror this morning and adding the bandana style print silk scarf draped at her neck. She'd pivot and admire the effect.

Behind her Ruth was making a silly face and Mandy, working the computer, peeked around her screen to wink at me. I quickly squelched my grin as Kim pulled me to the counter to show me what she'd spread out there. The plat map again.

"I talked to Eleanor, and she is still planning on keeping Harmony House out of the hands of any interested developers. I felt a hesitation on her part to let me know what she planned to do with it. Would she stay living there? Would she move to the old place? Or sell it and the lumber mill land above it? The Mill House! Oh my gosh, I just had a creative idea! A great name! The Mill House Estates! Just think. I must make a note of that. But after talking with you today...oh and I want to compliment you on your appearance. The way you casually swoop your gorgeous gray hair up into that bun. Fits perfectly with that stylish blue wrap coat and those gray jeans fit you to a T. I wish I had your tall figure." Kim giggled. "Me..." She kicked up one leg and rested her foot on a low display table. "I need these four inches to fake it."

"Ah, hi Kim," I said as she paused to take a breath, get her leg down, and straighten her figure-hugging sheath. "What was it you wanted to talk to me about."

I didn't dare look at Ruth or I would burst out laughing.

"I sensed your surprise at hearing Alan Morris's connection to my real estate dealings here. I just couldn't live with myself if I didn't assure you, I'm aware of your growing concerns about Paul's accident and how his businesses are held and funded, bought and sold."

Ruth was now doing a soft shoe shuffle off to the back room, which had been the original darkroom. Mandy managed to keep a straight face but signaled she'd interrupt if I needed help. I did a palm down wave at my hip. This chattering woman in front of me might actually, and unexpectedly, contribute to the case.

"Stuart explained that he found out you and Jeff haven't yet ruled Paul's death accidental. It worried him that I was getting caught up with some unsavory business. I assured him I may appear to be a scatter brain for want of a better word, but that under this," she jabbed a lacquered fingernail into her chestnut waves, "Is girl power. Hear me roar and all that. So, what more do you know?"

I was surprised by the screeching halt to her ramblings. Oh but patience Jackie, Kim has not finished talking.

"Today I am offering any help I can give to solve this mystery. I have worked primarily with Alan, but there are others looking at the property and I am the one they call. Word gets around. I could funnel any information to you. Or should I offer this help directly to the police? It's just that Eleanor mentioned how much she appreciated you being here to help her."

Mandy spun her computer screen so I could see it. The photograph of Kim's group was up and when I put two and two together, I quickly said, "Yes Kim. I believe there is a way you can help. Thank you so much for offering. Can you identify the people that appeared with you in a photograph?"

I swear I saw Kim's shoulders straighten as she said, "Certainly. May I see the photo?"

My phone dinged. I saw it was a text. Mandy stood and cleared her throat.

"You must excuse me. I need to take Libby out for a walk and grab a soda." As she walked by me, she whispered, "Look at it."

It was a cropped image from the more expansive view I'd taken on Saturday. I did a few taps and slides to fake out Kim into thinking I was digging through data on my phone, which is what Mandy had been thinking too. Smart girl. Keep things simple and clean. I held my cell up to Kim. "These people."

"Why that's me. And Alan I believe. It's sort hard to tell with the branches and leaves in the way. And that's Melody and Chelsea." Kim cut herself short as though she just realized something. "Where did you get that photo from?"

I didn't miss a beat, though I almost choked when I heard that the other woman in the photograph was Chelsea's mother and that she was in town. "It was sent to me." Not a lie. Mandy had just sent it. I knew I'd want to tread lightly here based on Kim's reaction.

"By who?"

I avoided answering her by saying, "I could tell it was you because you are always so coordinated in your dress. And the dabbles of sunlight against that stunning peach linen sheath caught my eye."

Kim seemed to relax her defenses again.

I continued. "I recognize Chelsea, but to be honest I wasn't sure of the other two. Possible buyers for the property? This looks like it was taken at the Harmony House."

"Yes, you're right. I was there on last Saturday showing it to him. I had Chelsea's permission and her mom just happened to be in town. For the wedding I suppose. Actually, I sort of have carte blanche there at Harmony House because I'm working with the land deal. I remember the day because I ended up changing out of that peach dress to go out for dinner later. Linen can be such a pain. But it is so stylish. Now they have those amazing pseudo fabrics, faux linen and pleather. So many options."

"Agreed! You are a powerhouse realtor Kim, that's for sure. So now that Eleanor is deciding to keep the house and grounds, can you show me some of those other perspective sites buyers are looking at."

The misdirection worked and Kim strode over to the spread-out plat map. Mandy came to my rescue again when my cell phone rang.

"Excuse me Kim. This is a call I have to take." I proceeded with a brief chat with Mandy who had just left to walk Libby. All Kim heard was me say was, "Okay then, sure. Let me say goodbye to someone here and I'll call you back in a few minutes and give you that information."

I clicked off on the call. "I'm sorry Kim, but I have to get back to this person shortly. Could give me a brief overview of all this? I don't know how you keep track of all the maneuverings. Guess you just have that type of brain. I think my left-brain functions better."

I let Kim's puzzled look slide by as I pointed at the salvage yard area. "You said this area was one possibility. I think it has great potential too. Based on your assessment of course. I'd never have figured it out myself."

Ruth returned to the front area and was sticking her finger in her throat. Was I overdoing it? Would Kim start to suspect I was egging her on?

"Are Arthur Cutter and the farmer willing to sell?" I asked.

"I'm working on them. When Melody mentioned the possibility of combining some other parcels a light bulb went off in my head. I got right on it that day. In fact, the dinner I mentioned having to change my dress for, was with the farmer and his wife. To pitch the idea to them. Melody said she knew Arthur Cutter and would feel him out about it. And that's why you saw me earlier with Scott today. I wanted his opinion as well."

"You are a mover and shaker I've got to say. Did Melody get back to you with good news on the salvage yard property?"

"Last I heard she was going there on Monday as soon as the place opened. She seemed very eager to help me. Hmm…I haven't heard from her though."

"She doesn't live here in Harmony?"

"Oh goodness no. Like I said I believe she came in for the wedding. My meeting her at the house was random. In fact, I must call Chelsea and get her mother's phone number. I'm glad I could help you with identifying that group of people. But you never said why you wanted to know."

Think quick Jackie. Come up with a plausible reason.

But before I could speak, Kim said, "Oh never mind Jackie. I appreciate you reminding me about the salvage yard property." She leaned in near me as though to offer me confidential information. "Between you and me, that Melody seemed off. She's had recent Botox work done including her lips, one of those walk-in places I would imagine. Not that I'm against trying to keep a youthful appearance, but good god you've got to go to the best, or it ends up looking hideous. And OMG she had this god-awful pink lipstick on. Put that look on a face above those obviously fake boobs, not a good idea." She leaned her head and tilted her chin up, catching a reflection of herself in the window. "Maybe I shouldn't be so snarky. Well, off I go. Glad I caught up with you again!"

"Glad you did too," I called after her.

If only she knew how very glad I was.

CHAPTER TWENTY-THREE

Ruth bowed toward me. "Masterful Jackie. Simply masterful."

"You heard all that?"

"I did. I can't believe Melody is back in town. Do you think Eleanor knows?" Ruth asked.

"I don't think so. But some other things make sense now. Pieces of the puzzle are falling in place."

"Your curiosity is legendary," Ruth said with a knowing laugh. "And my dear great-niece, if you ever find yourself needing more information on the real estate side of things, my friends at Shady Pines love a good mystery and have their ears to the ground. Plus friends in high places. Just sayin'!"

"Thank you, Aunt Ruth, I will keep that in mind. Do you remember Melody?" I asked.

"Not really. She wasn't here very long. But Mandy might know something. She went to school with Chelsea and they hung out once in a while."

"That's a good idea. I'll peek outside and see if I can catch her and Libby."

I gave Aunt Ruth a hug. She was the best.

*M*andy and Libby were on the bench outside the gas station. The yellow crime scene tape still blocked the repair bays.

"I have to thank you for your quick thinking just now. It really helped me avoid explaining too much to Kim."

"You're welcome," Mandy said. "Did she help you with figuring out what's going on?"

"Her comments added to my knowledge. Now I just need to piece a few more things together. Ruth said you might know Chelsea."

"I do. Went to high school with her. Billy too." She turned to look at the station. "What a sad way to die. All alone late at night. But I guess you can say it was quick."

"So you knew Billy too?"

"Sure. He was one of those cute bad boys in town. You know what I mean? Plus, a gear head I guess they called it. He loved to work on cars and had a sweet motorcycle as soon as he got his driver's license."

I smiled remembering a high school crush I'd had. "I think I do. Every generation has those cute bad boys as you called him."

Mandy laughed. "My mom and her older sisters talk about Elvis and all the edgy stuff he did."

"And of course, James Dean. Or at least his persona as an actor. Hot stuff for those times."

"So many of the guys here like to hunt and fish like my husband Matt. I'm not big into the hunting thing but his dad gets some cool sightings on his trail cameras. Even wolves and sometimes big cats like panthers and cougars."

"Wow I didn't know those were still in the state. I remember hearing about sightings over the years but few and far between. Suppose they are caught on those trail cameras often enough though."

"Yep. A lot of them move and feed at night so it's not as rare as you might think. In fact, when I read today's article about the accident, I asked Matt and Scott to see if they knew of anyone in the area with a trail camera. It seemed like a possibility that someone's camera might have captured images related to the accident."

"Smart idea Mandy," I said. "Good thinking."

Mandy bent to pat Libby's head as she stared at the garage again. "Do you think his death was accidental?"

"Don't you?"

She reached for the iced soda sitting next to her, seeming to weigh her answer. "I heard Billy and Chelsea had something going on for a while. Her mother really damaged Chelsea, leaving her like she did. I remember seeing this photo of Melody that Chelsea carried around. It was all worn down, tattered. I always thought that's why she did drugs, it was something to escape into."

"That had to be rough. But she's clean now right?"

Mandy shrugged. "Don't see her much now anymore."

"I'm glad you came in today so we could meet too. And I'm so glad you are excited about working with Ruth. Maybe we could talk some more in the morning. Together we can bring my aunt into the 21st century."

Mandy stood and reached to untangle Libby's leash that had wrapped around the bench legs. In the shuffle her drink got knocked over and the lid popped off, the straw dangling out of it.

An image like that flashed across my mind. "If you'll excuse me, there's someone I have to catch up with. See you tomorrow."

. . .

*D*arn I was too late. The dog lunged at the locked gates, snarling and snapping at me. "Easy Spike. It's just me. Is your owner around?" But my sweet talk did nothing to make him quiet down. It was apparent the place was closed up for the day. The padlock rattled against the wire gate as Spike leaped against it again. "Okay! Okay! I'm leaving."

Where to next? What proof did I need? And how could I get it? I got back in my car and took off for the Riverview Motel. Jeff called while I was on my way there.

"How's your day going detective Parker?"

"Jeff, listen up. Can you do me a favor? A big favor? I'm on my way to Wanda's now. But it would be a huge help to me if you could catch up with Scott."

I quickly explained what Mandy had told me. It was a long shot, but it might make all the difference in helping me prove my case. He agreed.

When I told Wanda what I needed from her she sprang into action, pulling up the security video from Saturday night. "You know Jeff has been here to view this right?"

"I know, but we've gathered a few more pieces of evidence and are looking at things from a little different angle now."

The film shows Alan being dropped off by Paul just as Jeff said. "Keep running it please."

There were some other cars pulling and guests entering their rooms for the night. Then I saw what I was looking for. At 11:36 a figure walked toward the office from behind the cottages. That's just as Nadine described, only she wasn't coming from the river area.

"This person," I tapped the screen, "came in for a replacement key. Do you have cameras showing the back area of the cottages?"

"No, it's on my endless to do list. What are you thinking friend? I can see that gleam in your eye."

"Wanda, I have an idea what's been going on around here and I could use your help. Are you up for it?"

Wanda clapped her hands. "Just like the old days only I would ask that question of you! Yes, I am up for it. Tell me what you need me to do."

CHAPTER TWENTY-FOUR

*T*he Wildwood Supper Club was quiet, a normal late Tuesday evening. That's the way I wanted it. Eleanor and Chelsea sat at a corner table near the door to the kitchen. Wanda and I joined them.

I knew our appearance caught Chelsea by surprise, but Eleanor said, "I'm so glad you could make it. Chelsea dear, I hope you don't mind, but I wanted to have Jackie join us. She's been so helpful to me over these past days."

"It's been my pleasure Eleanor. I know you and Ruth have enjoyed a long friendship so when you asked me, I was honored to help."

Wanda said, "And I'm glad you agreed to let me join you. I didn't get to see much of Jackie on this visit and I'd been looking forward to being with her tonight too, so it all worked out. Right Chelsea?"

Chelsea nodded, but her anxious look told me this wasn't what she'd expected. We ordered drinks and appetizers.

Chelsea seemed to relax.

"Did you grandmother tell you the autopsy results came in?" I asked between bites of a deep-fried cheese curd.

"No, she didn't," Chelsea said, looking to Eleanor. "Did they find traces of arsenic?"

"Yes, they did. But you'll never believe where the arsenic came from. The well water at the Mill House." Eleanor shook her head. "Crazy hah?"

"Really? So not from mint leaves?" Chelsea asked.

I stepped in. "No. They found long term exposure in a hair sample."

Chelsea said, "I'm relieved it wasn't what I'd suspected. I feel embarrassed about even suggesting that."

"Did Jeff get to look over those photos from Arthur Cutter? Did someone tamper with Paul's car so he would have an accident?" Eleanor asked, though I had already given the answer.

"Now that's a puzzler. Because I took photos of the car's undercarriage at the accident scene. And darn if the damage Cutter's photos showed wasn't on the car at that time. Jeff talked with Mr. Cutter today after reviewing both sets of photos. It's looking like he might have purposely done damage to the car after it arrived at his salvage yard Monday morning."

Chelsea took a deep swallow but kept her eyes on the drink she was holding.

Wanda asked, "Why on earth would he do that? I hope my cousin gets the truth out of him. No tampering with the car but tampering with evidence. And comparing the photos proved it?"

"It is certainly looking that way. Plus, Arthur Cutter had a great deal of other information," I said as I reached for another cheese curd while keeping an eye on Chelsea's reaction. She's trying very hard to not pay attention.

But at the next comment from my conspirator Wanda, Chelsea couldn't pretend anymore.

"It was nice to see your mother made it in for a visit. Do you have her phone number? I didn't realize it was her right away when she registered at the Riverview. But she left something behind. I must have gotten the wrong phone number from her when she checked in."

Chelsea almost choked. She didn't answer Wanda.

Eleanor said, "Chelsea honey, you didn't tell me your mother was in town."

After a short coughing spell, Chelsea said, "I know

you don't like her Grandma. But she wanted to surprise you and come to the wedding."

Eleanor said, "I see." She took a sip of her martini. "Today when Jeff and Jackie came over, they asked me if you ever found Paul's cell phone. I said we didn't have it. They were able to get his call records from his secretary. Amazing how so much information is in those computers. The records show Paul called the house after he dropped Alan off. I hope his calling didn't mean he took his eyes off the road and skidded down that embankment."

I took over. "The call lasted a couple of minutes, so he spoke to someone in the house."

"You told me and Chief of Police Mathis, that there were no calls that night Chelsea. Are you sure? I can't imagine who else would have answered at that hour," Eleanor said.

Wanda cued up her line. "Do you think he survived the crash and was calling for help?"

Eleanor gasped. "I hadn't thought of that. Do you think that's possible given what the autopsy revealed?" She turned to Chelsea. "I didn't finish sharing the details with you dear. Paul survived the car accident."

Chelsea slumped. Her breathing quickened.

Wanda patted her hand. "Are you alright Chelsea?" You don't look well."

Now Eleanor's demeanor changed. "Chelsea, I'll ask again and if you ever loved me, you'll tell me the truth. Did you speak to Paul at 11:04 on Saturday evening?"

We all sat waiting for Chelsea to speak.

Eleanor asked again. "Now Chelsea. I'm giving you a chance to explain to me. Please take it."

"Paul called that night," Chelsea finally said. She turned to me, a pleading look in her eye. "I'm so sorry I lied to the Chief and to you Jackie, but I thought no one would know and what would it matter anyway?"

There was an awkward pause until I said, "Go on."

And she did. The words spilled out. "I answered the phone. Paul said he wasn't hurt. He'd slid off the road and was caught up in his seat belt and couldn't get out. He was apologetic for calling and bothering us. He'd tried Alan's cell, but it must have been on a *do not disturb* mode. He told me not to wake you Grandma. I swear."

Eleanor glanced at me. She slowly shook her head, realizing what was coming. "Go on Chelsea."

"He didn't know the motel number. Could I call the motel and have them ring Alan's room? He could come and help untangle him. I asked Paul where he was and he said he'd gone off the road by a big yellow rock outcropping, not far from the motel. I swear he was even laughing Grandma! He said he was so embarrassed.

But he was fine. He didn't want to make a scene on the eve of his wedding he said."

Wanda took over at this point. "But you didn't call the motel as he directed you. We have no records of that."

Chelsea's tears came now. "I don't know why I called my mother instead. She was staying at the Riverview too. She knew Alan and could knock on his door. I thought that together they could help Paul."

Behind Chelsea's back, Jeff stepped out of the kitchen where he'd been listening to our conversation. She didn't see him.

"Paul told me he loved me, and he was glad that tomorrow we'd officially be family." At this point Chelsea was sobbing and quiet tears rolled down Eleanor's cheeks.

"What did your mother say when you spoke to her?" I asked.

"My mother said of course my love, you were right to call me. I begged her, Mom you promise you'll wake Alan and give him the message? Yes, my love I will she said, now don't you worry, Alan and I will get him out of the vehicle. She asked me how to find the car. You just let me handle this she said. My friend Arthur can tow the car out in the daylight. I thought I did the right thing."

"Why didn't you tell me all this?" Eleanor asked.

"I didn't want to wake you Grandma. Paul said not to wake you. That you'd just worry and there was nothing you could do. I knew Alan and Mom would help Paul. Alan was his friend. He'd be sure Paul was okay. And Sunday you and Paul would marry, and I could introduce him to Mom and surprise you."

"But he died Chelsea. And we didn't marry. What else have you kept from me about this?"

"Nothing. I swear. When I took you in for a makeup and hair appointment and was told about Paul having died in an accident, I was as shocked as everyone else. When I watched his car being towed by Billy along Main Street, I couldn't believe it. What had happened? Where had I failed? My mother didn't answer my calls. And Alan showed up for the ceremony as if nothing had happened."

"You should have told me the truth. I believe Chief Mathis has something to tell you now."

Chelsea's eyes flew wide-open when Jeff stepped forward and pulled a chair up to our table to sit down. "Chelsea, Paul's death wasn't the result of the accident. But of course, you knew that. The autopsy revealed he died of asphyxiation. He was murdered."

"Murdered? Nooo…oh god no please no." Chelsea's whispered as the news sunk in.

Eleanor knew what was coming, so she wrapped her arms around her granddaughter.

"And we are charging your mother with that murder. The police in Greensville are holding her," Jeff said.

Chelsea pulled out of Eleanor's arms. "What? My mother?" With frightened eyes she pleaded with Eleanor. "Grandma, no. That can't be true." Then she spun toward Jeff. "You can't be right. She loved me. She'd never do something like that to hurt me. You've got it wrong." She grabbed my arm, "Jackie, tell them they're wrong. Please someone, stop this."

"I'm afraid it's true Chelsea. We have just received the final piece of video evidence to confirm our suspicions."

"You'll have to come with me now Chelsea," Jeff said.

"What? Why? Grandma help me. I didn't do anything thing. I'm sorry I didn't tell you, but I didn't know everything."

"That may be true, but you didn't tell us the truth about what you knew. You are being charged with obstruction of justice."

CHAPTER TWENTY-FIVE

*J*eff led Chelsea out of the supper club. What Melody did, not once, but twice to her daughter was unspeakable. The destructive powers love has.

Wanda was the first to speak. "What a sad story. Why would Melody have done that?"

"Greed. Plain and simple," I said. "She saw one last hope that, instead of the most desirable piece of property, the developer would buy land that included the Cutter Salvage Yard. She'd schemed with Cutter for months. They both would profit if they could have pulled it off. With Paul out of the picture, she thought Eleanor and Chelsea would stay at the mansion. She was desperate for that to happen. Cutter, with an offer of lenience for his part of tampering with evidence, told Jeff the entire story."

"But wouldn't that be his word against her's?"

"We needed one last piece. Jeff texted me just before we got here that the trail camera captured Melody in the act. But it wasn't very clear. We're hoping they can enhance it."

Wanda said, "I still don't get it. If it's a blurry figure on film, what makes you so sure it's her and not maybe Alan?"

"I spoke to Nadine this afternoon. She told me about a woman needing an extra key late Saturday night. The guest's story was she'd walked down to the river and lost hers. But remember when I wanted to see the film again today?"

Wanda nodded. "I do. We saw Alan on it when Paul dropped him off."

"Right. What we didn't see was a woman walking across the parking lot, which she would have done if she came from the river. The camera shows a woman approaching the offices shortly after midnight from the area of the cottages."

"Ah, now I get it. The lost key woman was Melody. That key Jeff found at the crash site was her's. She dropped it in the dark and had to get another at the motel office."

"There was one more very incriminating information clear on the trail camera film." I moved my cupped hands over my chest in a wide motion. "No way Alan would have had a pair of those!"

Wanda almost burst out laughing but stifled it out of respect for Eleanor.

I said, "As to why Chelsea couldn't imagine her mother doing that, I think it's as simple as a constant ache for your mother's love. When it seems in reach again, there's no end to what a hurting child will believe and what she will blindly deny."

Wanda said, "Eleanor, I'm so sorry. You've given her everything you could."

"Thank you, Wanda. I'm grateful you and Jackie agreed to meet me here with Chelsea. I couldn't have done this on my own. You're right Jackie. Chelsea got caught up in wanting her mother's love. When you explained to me what you had discovered, I knew Chelsea had to be confronted. And I also knew how crushed she'd be when her mother's true selfish plot was revealed. But I'll hire a good attorney and hopefully get her charge reduced to a misdemeanor."

"Jackie, was there anything else you discovered that pointed you to Melody?" Wanda asked.

"A few things. But a small tiny detail sort of pulled it all together for me...lipstick on a straw! Monday morning, when I went out to the salvage yard to see Paul's wrecked car, I noticed a lipstick stained straw."

"And you knew it wasn't Arthur's color?" Eleanor said.

I was happy to hear Eleanor crack a joke. "Right! Then this morning two things occurred. Kim, with her attention to style, mentioned a notable color of pink lipstick Melody wore. When I randomly saw a straw in Mandy's soda, the connection clicked. That pink was the color of the lipstick on the straw at Cutter's."

"Good eyes Jackie," Wanda said.

"Your cousin, our Chief of Police has good eyes too," Eleanor said. "I don't know if you knew about this Wanda, but Arthur told Chelsea and I that someone had tampered with Paul's car. He strongly suggested it caused the accident."

"I heard that. Remember you told us at the Cut-n-Curl this morning. Jeez that seems like a week ago," Wanda said.

"It sure does," Eleanor said. "But today I learned that photos Jackie took at the scene showed no damage. So that means Arthur Cutter tried to shift the blame for the accident to Billy by implying he'd purposely tinkered with the car. But Arthur himself was the one who messed with it, trying to point away from him and Melody."

"She figured no one would ever know. They'd just attribute his death to the car crash." I shook my head. "Did I tell you that I saw Melody Monday night? Course I didn't know who she was then. Today, when Val later told me about seeing a woman talking with Cutter at Shorty's Monday evening, I remembered. Monday evening, after visiting with Ruth's friends at Shady Pines, I was relaxing on the studio's balcony and took note of a woman leaving Shorty's. I watched her walk past me and on down Main Street. Now I know it was, Melody. She could have been going to Billy's garage. The lights were still on there. I've noticed Billy working into the evening before. Since the crime scene tape is up and the site has been untouched, Jeff is going to try to lift fingerprints in the morning. I have a strong suspicion they will be Melody's."

"Are you suggesting she knocked over the carjack on purpose?" Wanda asked. "I'll believe anything at this point. Good detective work, Jackie."

"I guess my mind doesn't work like yours Jackie. Why would she do that?" Eleanor asked.

I reminded her of the call from Arthur Cutter and how he'd pointed at Billy being a suspect in tampering with Paul's car.

"Now I get it. Arthur didn't know other photos would disprove what he tried to show in his photographs." Eleanor closed her eyes, shaking her head side to side. "And I even said to go ahead and start taking the car apart."

Wanda said, "So taking out Billy would take out the person they accused of doing it. And she would make it look like an accident again."

"Or so she thought," I said. "Cutter could see all the evidence puzzle pieces falling into place, he sang like a bird when Jeff confronted him."

The three of us closed up the Wildwood Supper Club. Wanda asked Eleanor if she preferred we give her a ride instead of driving home alone.

"I'll be fine. I'm sticking to the main road." She gave me a big hug. "I owe you Jackie. What you've done to help me has been priceless. How can I ever repay you?"

"It's nothing Eleanor. I'm just so sorry the way this whole thing came down. I sure wish I would be handing you wedding photographs instead of just those staging photographs I gave you."

"Speaking of that. I will continue on with the plans Paul and I made. Harmony House and the grounds looked so beautiful in your photographs. I just can't imagine it all broken up for some condos or a resort. I'm going to donate it to the Village of Harmony if they'll take it."

"That's wonderful to hear!" Wanda said.

"I'll sell some acreage more distant from the house, up and over toward the old lumber mill grounds. We'll see. But I feel good, I have made the right decision. Please stop in and say hello next time you're in town Jackie."

"I will Eleanor. You take care."

"Now what are your plans my friend?" Wanda asked as I headed toward the motel to drop her off.

"Well I'm staying the night then heading back to Chicago in the morning. This has been a crazy few days."

uth and I drank our morning coffee on the balcony. Libby joined us, curling up at my feet. I did most of the talking as Ruth insisted, I fill her in on all the details of last night.

"Well now if that don't beat all. Small town life, heh?"

"Wanda wants me to do some shots of the motel for a calendar or more publicity. Do you think Mandy would like to help me with that? I could give her some ideas and then let her have at it. That would mean I wouldn't have to drive over as often to catch just the right weather."

"You know, I bet she'd love that. In fact, here she comes. Why don't you talk to her about it?"

"I will. You stay up here and enjoy your coffee."

I went over my idea with Mandy and she jumped at

the chance to learn more about photography. "Mandy, did you ever think of buying a business like this? I mean you seem to enjoy it, and it would allow you to have something to build and grow for your future."

"There's no way Matt and I could afford this. But I love working here and I hope Ruth keeps it. I mean if she sells the building where would she go?"

"She'd like to move to Shady Pines."

"But this business has been around for decades. Hey how about you take it over? Make it a gallery for your work? And other photographers could sell here to. I'm planning on learning to frame so I could do that upstairs or in the old darkroom. We could be like partners! And gosh if you taught me more about the actual photography skills, I could keep up that end of it. I'm sure Matt and his dad would do a great remodeling. Like over here..." She walked around the first-floor space tossing out ideas and visions.

I saw what she was thinking about. Maybe she was on to something. I could afford it. And it would be an offer that Ruth could see her way to accept. Definitely something to think about. Yes, this might work.

"Let me think about it," I said with a new confidence that Parker Photography would survive and thrive.

Mandy smiled. "I will."

Ruth and Libby came downstairs. "What are you going to think about, Jackie?"

I held a finger up to my lips. Shhh, I signaled to Mandy.

Ruth noticed. "Jacqueline Parker, what is going on?"

Mandy quickly said, "Jackie and I are going to work together on some publicity for Wanda. Maybe even a calendar. I'm going to take photographs out there if you'll let me borrow your equipment and then upload them to a website where Jackie can critique them."

"More with the website stuff. I'm getting behinder and behinder on that stuff every day! Come on Libby, let's walk Jackie out to her car."

In a few minutes I was waving goodbye. I took a photo of Aunt Ruth waving back, just as I'd done so often before.

Hannah called out from across the street. "I will keep my eyes open for some great old frames for you Jackie. Have a safe drive home."

"Thanks Hannah."

I grabbed a coffee at Murphy's for the drive ahead. Grace was working. "Our son told us what an extraordinary effort you put into helping Eleanor. I wanted to thank you. She's been so kind and supportive to us in establishing our business. We're all glad you helped solve that one."

Stuart tapped on the window of the Harmony Hills Happening office, adding a wave and a smile to my departure.

As I was getting back in the car, I saw Scott's pickup drive by. He gave a little toot. I smiled. Maybe remodeling the studio wouldn't be a bad idea if it meant working with him.

The drive back to Chicago gave me time to mull over possibilities regarding Parker Photography. If Mandy was as good of an employee as she appeared, it might work. But partner would be even better! She'd have more invested. I wouldn't have to be tied down here in Harmony. Ruth could move to Shady Pines and I could still travel for the work I did. Plus, it meant keeping my loft and my independence in Chicago.

This time leaving Harmony was just a little harder than usual. The itch I'd get to be back in the big city hadn't happened.

I had some thinking to do.

he End

Murder in a Dark Gloom...the next Parker Photography Cozy Mystery Series...

Chapter One

"This is quite the soiree," my Aunt Ruth said as we turned into the long drive and approached Harmony House on its perch above the river.

"Think they'll have a red carpet rolled out for us?" I teased.

"Well, they might. I heard there will be a Senator in attendance, and someone said press from Milwaukee will even be here," Ruth said. "Stuart Walters will be in hog heaven writing this up for our local paper."

"It'll be good to see him again." I pulled up in front of the mansion to drop Ruth off. Uplighting thrown against the tall sturdy oaks was magical. Luminaries glowed on the walkway to the front porch.

This fundraiser was a big event for the little village of Harmony. My memories of only a few months ago flooded back. It would be good to see Eleanor Harmony again. The last time I'd been with her had not been pleasant for either of us. This would be quite a different scene.

Ruth looked lovely in her formal gown. I sensed her excitement. She and her friends at Shady Pines had decided to pull out all the punches to attend this once in a decade event. They were making the most of it! Dorothy's granddaughter piled them all in her minivan, and they traveled together to a dress shop in Madison to find evening wear. Then today they spent time together at Val's Cut-n-Curl for manicures, pedicures, and hair-styling. Wish I could have been a fly on the wall there.

"I'll park and be right up. You go on ahead," I said as Ruth stepped out and adjusted her dress. "By the way did I tell you how gorgeous you look?"

She grinned at me and did a twirl on the sidewalk. "Old lady still has it." She walked off with an extra wiggle of her behind. Spunky for an octogenarian. I hope I inherited some of that through my Parker genes.

I turned my SUV's wheels to pull back out when a loud honk alerted me to the fact that a car had pulled up right next to me.

"Okay, okay. Didn't see you," I mumbled as I waited for them to move. In my side mirror I saw a foot in a high heeled red shoe slip out, followed by a long leg peeking out of the slit in an elegant red gown. The passenger stood and paused to collect herself, surveying the scene before taking the arm of a man who'd been waiting to greet her. They air kissed as the car she'd arrived in began to pull away.

The chauffeur nodded at me as he drove past. This was more than a little historical society fundraiser. One never saw chauffeured cars around Harmony unless it was a wedding party being driven between the church and the ballroom.

In my business as a photographer I've attended many formal events, not only in Chicago where I live, but around the world. I was glad I'd chosen my long satin navy blue skirt, instead of the calf length black one I'd also packed. I tended to dress to blend in, not stand out like the woman in the red gown. But that kind of person always did add a bit of spice to a party.

The people of Harmony were surprised, but excited, when Eleanor Harmony, after losing her fiancé on the eve of their wedding, decided to donate her family mansion to the village and move into another smaller home where her parents had been raised. Downsizing they call it. Eleanor was closer to Aunt Ruth's age, but even me, in my 60s, could understand the sense of that move.

The Historical Society outdid themselves with this fundraiser to get the mansion and grounds up to modern-day standards. Ruth had been telling me about all the hard work put into making this evening special. And their efforts obviously paid off.

Familiar faces greeted me as I entered. Hannah and her husband Mark, owners of the local antique shop, waved from the top of the grand staircase. Ruth told me they had been hired to catalog and appraise the antiques here. My lifelong friend, Wanda Mathis, took a champagne glass from a waiter's tray. She gave me an okay finger circle and quick point toward the champagne glasses still on the tray. I nodded and watched her smoothly grab another glass from the waiter and begin to head over to me.

"Jackie!"

I spun to see who had screamed my name. Hurrying toward me was a vision in another stunning red gown, with her thick chestnut hair piled up in an intricately woven crown on top of her head. Kim Walters, local real estate agent extraordinaire, practically jumped into my arms. Luckily, I braced myself.

"You did come! Hooray! I'm so happy. When I noticed you donated a portrait sitting to the silent auction, I just knew I'd be bidding on that one. I mean, who wouldn't want to sit for such a famous photographer? Do you believe the turnout for this gala?" She spun around, throwing her hands in the air. "Why everyone who is anyone is here."

She hadn't changed. And tonight she was in her element. Kim was the go to realtor for Harmony. A reputation she deserved and made well known to anyone within earshot.

"You look gorgeous, Kim. That rich red color is perfect for you. Is your husband Stuart here?"

She looked around the room. "Hmm...he's here somewhere doing his newspaper thing. It'll be a bigger edition on this Tuesday. Harmony hasn't seen an event like this in a long time. And I'm just so glad to be a part of it. I donated the pamphlets explaining the vision for Harmony House."

"That's very generous of you," I said. "I'll have to be sure to pick one up."

Kim reached inside her evening bag. "Oh darn, I don't have anymore. But they're spread around all over. I had your Aunt Ruth do new headshots of me for my ad on the back. Have to stay current. Will you look at her!"

Kim took my shoulder and forced me to look toward the parlor area.

"Who Kim?" I asked, praying Wanda would get here soon and rescue me.

"Luella Hagge, in a red dress almost identical to mine. I could wring her neck," Kim said through gritted teeth.

It was the woman from the limo. "Kim," I said, extracting myself from her grasp. "It really doesn't look much like yours. Besides, you wear red much better than she does."

The remark calmed her down. "Thank you, Jackie.

That compliment means a great deal. In fact, I traveled to your stomping grounds in Chicago to find just the right dress for this evening. You look lovely as well... Vera Wang? Oh, and guess what? Alan Morris is going to be here. Remember him? He's still involved with the land deal for the resort." Kim took a breath to straighten her shoulders and stretch her neck up to search over the crowd. "I must make sure to catch up with him."

I saw a chance to make my break. "If you'll excuse me, Kim, I see a glass of champagne with my name on it."

She touched my arm and in a soft conspiratorial voice said, "I'm glad we solved the mystery of Paul's death with you. What a tragedy. And to think, I provided the final link so the arrest could be made."

She waited. Obviously expecting recognition from me.

"It was a tragedy. I'm sure Eleanor appreciates your contribution to the investigation."

With a smug smile, she licked her lips and said, "Oh, and I hope you find Stu. See you later, I have to go make that bid on your donation!"

Wanda almost crashed into another guest as she made her way across the room. The older gentleman was light on his feet as he shuffled easily sideways and pulled his body out of her way to avoid a collision. Wanda flushed, acknowledging him with her open smile and an oops grimace. I watched them exchange a few words.

"Whew, that was close," she said, handing me a crystal champagne glass filled with bubbly and simultaneously raising hers for a toast. "Welcome back home, my friend. May Harmony's Historical Society rake in piles of dough tonight."

"This is amazing. Aunt Ruth told me how hard the committee has been working to pull this together."

"With a good haul tonight, they can get the place up and running soon. Have you seen the renderings of the proposed changes?" Wanda said.

"No, I haven't. Just got here. I dropped Aunt Ruth off before I parked, and I've already lost her."

"I saw you ran into Kim. You'll see her mug plastered all over the handouts she donated. But thankfully the renderings are a Kim free zone."

I followed Wanda. She wasn't easy to lose. Her typical style of choosing vivid colors and prints made her dress stand out in this crowd. Across the room, Scott Drake stood by three tripod display stands with proposed updates to the house and grounds exhibited on them. He pointed at specific items and seemed to be explaining them to the woman from the limo. Luella

Hagge hung on his every word. And practically leaning on him for support as she listened intently.

Wanda explained to me how they had plans to rent out the mansion and grounds for events, and have a barn area for school and scout groups to experience nature. "Eleanor has to be happy about her decision. Something like this is a once in a lifetime chance for a small village like Harmony to preserve and display its history."

Scott caught Wanda's eye and gave a wink. Luella noticed it and turned to glance at us before giving us a beauty pageant smile.

"It's a big deal. Lots of volunteers will be helping get the place ready," Wanda said.

"Is Drake Construction involved in the project?"

"Yes. Scott's been instrumental in pushing it forward. Eleanor didn't want to leave something to the society that needed a lot of updating, so Scott has been helping her upgrade some plumbing and electrical before she donated it. Now the society committee chose to keep him on to complete changes for them. Want to rescue him? Looks like he's stuck with Luella."

I'd met Scott Drake the last time I visited and found him very personable and easy on the eyes. And with that low, slow Sam Elliott voice, a joy to listen to. His daughter-in-law Mandy Drake was doing a great job working with my aunt in the Parker Photography studio. In fact, I needed to keep an eye out for her because I wanted to ask her something.

"Who is this Luella person? I noticed her arriving in a limousine," I whispered to Wanda.

"Of course, she would make an entrance like that. She likes attention. Like how her red gown screams *look at me*. Luella is the current head of the county's Building and Zoning Department. But she's running for DA against Len Lampert in a special election. Looks like she's campaigning hard for Scott's vote," Wanda said in a suggestive voice.

I didn't have to be asked twice to be part of this rescue mission. We wound our way through the crowd.

ABOUT THE AUTHOR

Suzanne Bolden is the pen name for Brenda Felber. Suzanne writes cozy mysteries for adults. While Brenda continues her Pameroy Mystery Series for middle-grade readers.

www.brendafelber.com

Please follow me on my Amazon Author Central Page to receive updates on new releases...

If you enjoyed *Captured on Camera*, please take a minute to leave a review as they help other readers discover books they would enjoy reading.

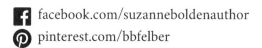 facebook.com/suzanneboldenauthor
pinterest.com/bbfelber

Made in the USA
Monee, IL
06 July 2021